GIVE ME HOPE - THE REASON SERIES BOOK 2

Zoey Derrick

GIVE ME HOPE

Zoey Derrick

COVER DESITE: Cover Designed by Rachel @ Parajunkee - www.parajunkee.net

EDITING: Completed with Sione Aeschliman of Sione Aeschliman LLC

ISBN: 0991525355
ISBN-13: 978-0991525355

Reason Series Reading Order:

Give Me Reason - Reason #1

Give Me Hope - Reason #2

Give Me Desire - Reason #3

Give Me Love - Reason #4

The REASON Series - Completed Collection

Other Works by Zoey Derrick

Finding Love's Wings

The Struggle Anthology

For Vickie - without your driving support, I might not have finished this.

The entire Reason Series is dedicated to all the men and women around the world who are or have been a victim of Domestic Violence.

One

"Let them in," I tell Red. The familiar hum in my back dulls out, and I take it to mean that there's no immediate danger. "I haven't a clue on earth why they're here, but let them in."

He turns for the door and opens it to reveal two men dressed in police uniforms. The man in front is about my height, stocky, and a little pudgy around the midsection. I estimate that he's well into his forties, with graying, short, military-style hair. He has a very intense look about him, like he's unsure of me, but he's confident in getting what he's after. The combination is strange, but he has a rather stoic, typically neutral expression.

There is another officer behind him and to his left who is much shorter but well-built and rather young.

Both men are very confident in their uniforms, and they both radiate authority. The intention is clear on their faces: They're out for information. But what?

"Mr. Blake?" The older one asks.

"Yeah, that's me. What can I do for you?"

"May we come in?"

I nod. They stalk into the room like giants, their boots echoing off the tile and entryway walls.

"I'm Detective Stevens, and this is Officer Ruiz. We are with the Minneapolis Police Department. We'd like to ask you a few questions, if you don't mind."

"Of course I mind, but I'm not going to stop you from asking."

Stevens's face remains impassive, and he is quick to continue with what he came here to do. "Would you please tell us what your car was doing on the corner of Lake and Chicago about thirty minutes ago?"

Vivienne's apartment. A sharp warning stab zings across my back, and I'm not sure I should trust these men. "Excuse me?"

"Doesn't seem like the type of neighborhood you'd usually be caught hanging out in," Stevens says, gesturing to the marble floor and the leather couches before turning his attention to his notepad.

I bristle at the word caught. "That really doesn't seem any of your business. Have I done something wrong? Broken any laws?"

Stevens looks up from his notepad. "We never said you did, we just want to know why you were there."

Thinking about Vivienne's apartment sends another sharp zing across my skin. Something is off. "I was... checking up on a friend."

Stevens's eyes widen slightly, and then a scowl forms. "Do you know Riley Bennett?" he asks sternly. Zing.

Riley Bennett. Why does that name ring bells? Something about that name... "No, I can't say that I do. Does he work for me?" I ask back.

"What about Rebecca Black?"

I shake my head.

"And lastly, Vivienne Callahan?"

All the breath in my lungs rushes out of my body. I feel my knees shake violently and I try to steady myself. The hum surges like a shock of electricity across my entire body, pulsing with each frantic beat of my heart. "Vivienne? What about Vivienne?" Then it dawns on me like a bolt of lightning. "Riley! Riley is Vivienne's ex-boyfriend. The bastard that put her in the hospital."

The cops look at each other, and Stevens turns back to me. He shifts his feet as he does, taking a rather defensive stance. "You know about that?"

I nod. "I..." I try to relax a little just so I can talk. "Can you tell me first if she's alright? Vivienne?"

Two

Officer Ruiz nods. "She's fine. Got home about half an hour ago." I feel a harder jolt across my back. Something is *definitely* off. "We're watching her apartment. Which is how we ended up here. Your black Mercedes was seen parked across Lake Street from her apartment. Then you left the area once she got off the bus and to her door."

I let the sense of relief flood over me, and I take a deep breath. I hadn't realized that my breathing was so slow and shallow. Emotions I don't understand wrack my body, mind and soul. I can't take it if I lose another--

I stop the thought short. I've had enough tragedy in my life. I can't even begin to think about losing Vivienne too.

I nod. It is difficult to form words with my throat still so tight. "I met Vivienne about two weeks ago at the diner. I was in that area attending a reception. I was hungry, so I stopped in. I met her then." No need to tell them that it wasn't my stomach that led me to the diner.

"I'd seen what kind of condition she was in, and I wanted to try and find a way to help her. A few days later I tried to help her by taking her to H.C.M.C., where she was seen by a Dr. Alston."

"Go on," Detective Stevens says, scribbling in his notebook.

I nod. "It turned out it wasn't the first time Vivienne had been Dr. Alston's patient. I eventually put two and two together. At some point that afternoon, I did or said something that upset Viv, and she threw me out of her room." That was probably one of the worst experiences of my life. I pushed her too hard, and she snapped. It is not an experience I want to have repeated anytime soon.

Detective Stevens smiles in a good-for-her way. "She seems the type."

I shake my head at the expression on his face and snort at his words. "You can say that again. Anyway, I made sure she was taken care of. Due to my being a major shareholder in the hospital, Dr. Alston agreed to keep in touch with me about her progress, and she was released the next morning. She wouldn't take money from me, but Dr. Alston was able to collect some cash from the hospital to help her out. I've stayed away from her since then. But I need to know she is safe, and I feel a sense of responsibility toward her to make sure it stays that way. Every night, I wait near her apartment until she gets home, and then I leave. Nothing more."

"A bit stalker-ish dontcha think?" The younger officer asks.

"Maybe, but she is a tiny little thing. She is about thirteen weeks pregnant, with no money, living in one of the roughest neighborhoods in Minneapolis. I worry about her safety." I sigh. "Is there a point to all of this, Detective?"

There is no immediate reply, but the less stoic expression on Stevens's face is telling me that he's deciding something. Whether or not he trusts me? I'm not sure I care, but it is rather obvious in his defensiveness regarding Vivienne that he too cares about her in some strange way. I take some comfort in that fact, all the while realizing that Vivienne is very easy to care about.

"Riley Bennett was released on bail last week." *Zing.* "We have reason to believe that he is looking for her." The sharp stab returns, and I know my face scrunches up. "We came here to find out whether there's a connection between you and Riley Bennett." He scowls slightly, scrutinizing my reaction. Reading me.

"I'll admit, my actions are probably a little over the top when it comes to Vivienne, but I'm not doing anything illegal." Technically. "And I'm certainly not in league with Riley."

He nods, accepting that I'm telling him the truth, and continues, "I spoke with her earlier today, let her know the situation, and she was willing to cooperate with the police presence. Officer Ruiz, Officer Hoffman and myself made our presence known at the diner by having dinner there tonight."

"That was nice of you." I try to smile, but something is off. I can't see it yet, but something.

"One of our detectives rode home on the bus with her tonight. He said that at first she seemed wary of him, but once he showed her his badge she relaxed a little bit."

Rage washes over me. "Why on earth are you trying to scare her half to death with shit like that?"

"We're doing our job, Mr. Blake. She needs to know we are there to protect her."

A sharp zing of pain stabs hard and fierce across my back. Jesus, what the hell is this all about? I don't understand it.

"She's had it hard enough as it is. You need to stop scaring her. She does not need to be worked up like this right now." Both the detectives look at each other, as if questioning my words. This makes my desire to be at the hospital tomorrow burn hotter. I need to know that she's safe, and I will do whatever it takes to make her see that. Is it possible that maybe, with all this going on, she will willingly let me help her? Let me protect her from Riley? That's assuming she needs protection from Riley. I have a distinct feeling that Riley might not be all she needs protection from.

I'm suddenly very curious as to what has led the police to this point. "What makes you think that he is after Vivienne?" I ask. They both look at each other, deciding. "Well?"

"Wednesday afternoon, Vivienne had a visit from an old mutual friend of hers and Riley's. When I spoke to Vivienne yesterday, she told me about that conversation. But we're still working on what transpired after this friend left the diner. Vivienne was under the impression that Riley was using her to get to Vivienne."

"Why the hell would she think that?"

"Because she told Vivienne that she was there to warn her about Riley." *Zing.*

Shit. I really don't like the sound of this. I have a sudden urge to drive over there and knock on her door.

But when the detectives leave a few moments later, the urge to drive to Vivienne's apartment subsides. I don't want another run-in with Stevens; plus, if she is safe in her apartment, then I do not want to scare her further by showing up in the middle of the night.

Three

I turn to Red. "Did she make it into her apartment tonight?"

"She did," he says back.

"Good." I'd only been home for all of five seconds when the cops showed up. I had a business meeting that ran over, so Red had gone to Vivienne's tonight in my place. "Anything unusual?"

"Not a thing, except the light over her front door was out. She didn't seem too bothered by it, and the bus driver hung around just a little longer than normal. I almost missed the drive-by timing." He smiles. "She was smirking at the car as I drove past."

"Even better. Maybe now she will be ready to talk to me."

He raises his eyebrows in a you've-lost-your-damn-mind kind of way. He's probably right.

There's something undeniably special about Vivienne, but I can't quite put my finger on it. Not yet. But eventually I will. I will find a way to do just that.

"I'll be in my office for a bit if you need me."

"Certainly, sir. Anything else?"

"No, not tonight. Thanks, Red."

"Anytime, sir."

I turn and head toward my office.

The police showing up here because of my car makes me question their motives altogether. What on earth is the connection between Vivienne, Riley and myself that they're seeing and I'm not?

Sitting down at my desk, I flick the mouse on my iMac, and the screen comes to life. The background comes up and I smile. It is a scanned copy of Baby Callahan's ultrasound image.

That baby is so unbelievably special, and Vivienne hasn't even begun to grasp that yet. Well, maybe she does a little now that she's had her ultrasound.

I can only imagine the emotional strain she's under, knowing that she's doing this alone. I'd really hoped to help her, maybe even be with her, if she'd have me. Be everything she needed me to be.

Until I met Vivienne I had no idea what love at first sight meant, but now I do. In more ways than one. I'd known when I was standing across the street from the diner with all those images flashing through my mind that there was something different about her, but I wasn't able to put my finger on it. When she was shaking from hunger and I told her that it wasn't just her I was worried about, I didn't realize what had come out of my mouth until after it had left. I had the fleeting thought that maybe she was pregnant, but it came and went so quickly that her telling me she was pregnant surprised me.

It was not what I'd expected to hear out of her mouth -- I was initially concerned that it was drug- or disease-related, and a pregnancy was the furthest thing from my mind -- but when she told me, it felt somehow familiar, like I'd already known.

I fell in love a second time when Dr. Alston raised her hospital gown, and there on her right hip was a heart-shaped birthmark. A mark that had become a legend in my family.

When I was a boy in our small town outside of Dublin, there was a crazy old lady who would walk past our house at the same time every day, muttering nonsense. My father said that she was just talking to herself, but each thing she said had something to do with one of us. It wasn't until we moved to Boston and my brother Shane was born that my parents started to believe there was something more to the old woman's mutterings.

"Light and darkness all at once," she used to say. Shane was born on the same day that my great-grandfather died.

Then my little brother, Ronin, came along. He was born with bright red hair and a pattern of freckles that formed a star under his right eye. This, too, the old woman had foretold.

Victoria's prophecy was the spookiest. The old woman had told my mother that they would have "a daughter of four," meaning fourth, and that she would be "frail and sickly, too", or something like that. When Victoria was born, she didn't leave the hospital until she was nearly six months old. I suppose some part of me expected that she'd die young, but of my whole family, Victoria and I are the only ones still living.

Though in Victoria's case, *alive* might be a better term. She resides in a state hospital in upstate New York -- one of the best. I wouldn't have it any other way. But I'm not sure she's really living in the sense of having a life of her own.

My prophecy went something like: "Alone he'll be, a wealth of three, a wife she'll be." There was a poem, too, but that's all that I really remember.

The prophecy, if it can be called that, alluded to a heart shape on her. It wasn't until we were in the hospital and Dr. Alston was getting ready to do the ultrasound that I saw it. There, over her right hip is that heart-shaped mark.

I only wish there was someone that I could talk to about all of this as it seems to slowly becoming reality.

Four

Thoughts of Vivienne bring me back to the reason I came in here in the first place.

Shaking my head of those thoughts, I turn to the computer; pull up Safari and type in *Rebecca Black*. There are a lot of women with that name, but none of the entries are recent.

I search instead for local crime reports from the last two days and find a *Star Tribune Online* article about a girl who was brutally murdered in South Minneapolis. Victim still unidentified.

My stomach turns, and the shivering sensations on my back intensify briefly. I peruse the rest of the article. The information it contains is weak and provides me with no real concrete proof that it has to do with the Rebecca Black the cops asked about. Though the location suggests it could be.

I go back to Google and search for Riley Bennett. These results seem more promising, and within a matter of minutes I discover a connection I no longer like -- a business relationship that will soon be severed. Riley Bennett is the son of Elton Bennett, CEO of Bennett and Lisbon Enterprises, a company that I do business with on a regular basis.

No longer. I will not stand side by side with a man that bails his kid out of jail after that kid viciously beats a girl for being pregnant with his child.

I grab my BlackBerry, pull up a contact and press send.

"Good evening, Mr. Blake. To what do I owe this pleasure?"

"Hi, Jack. I need you to put your research skills to work. Are you ready?"

"Absolutely. Fire away."

Not only will I sever my ties to Bennett and Lisbon, but I will bring Elton down in a fiery inferno. I'm not generally this vindictive, but damn it, this is Viv we're talking about.

When I'm done talking to Jack, I head for the bedroom and a shower. My back is starting to itch. That's odd. I try to scratch it, but its right in the middle of my back where I can't reach.

As my feet hit the bedroom carpet, I start shedding clothes, first unbuttoning the shirt and letting it slip from my shoulders onto the floor. Then off come the belt, pants and socks. Finally my boxer briefs hit the bathroom floor.

As I reach into the shower to turn the knob, something catches the corner of my eye.

I turn quickly but see nothing. It must be the stress. Maybe I'm even a little freaked out by the fact that Riley has been freed, and he's wormed his way into my unconscious mind.

I turn again and it's back. This time I turn slowly, hoping to catch sight of whatever it is. For a moment I see it in the mirror, faint before it disappears again. I turn my body so that my back is facing the mirror. I'm looking over my shoulder, and in an instant the old lady's words come flooding back to me.

> *An angel is he*
> *Alone in this world*
> *With the wealth of three*
> *He'll meet his true love*
> *Answering her song*
> *His wings he will grow*
> *His heart will respond*
> *Him she will follow*
> *His wife she will be*
> *Two joined making three.*

Jesus, I'm losing it, I swear to God. I'm seeing things, and now, all of sudden after twenty years that old lady's words come back to me.

Is it even possible that I am an angel? I thought angels were born of those that die and earn their right as angels. How is it that I'm walking this earth and can be an angel? 'Cause that makes a lot of sense, doesn't it?

Vivienne. How on earth does she fit into all of this? The heart on her hip, the birthmark. The need I feel of being around her.

What if all this is really coming true?

Five

My body is burning. The hum I've been experiencing of late has begun to burn across my entire body.

Opening my eyes, I look at the clock. Eight. I get up quickly, hoping that moving around will soothe the burning feeling, but it doesn't.

Last night's realization that something is changing in my body comes flooding back to me.

I'd never taken my family's story as anything more than gibberish until now. The story tells, in some mixed-up way, that I'm supposed to become an angel.

An angel is he...

I shake my head. Jesus, I'm losing it.

"I'm hardly pure enough to be an angel," I mutter as I shed the t-shirt I slept in and exchange it for a light gray undershirt and a gray button up dress shirt. I pull on my favorite pair of faded Wrangler jeans and slip on black socks and my black boots.

Every time I've seen Vivienne so far, I've been dressed in a suit. Not my usual attire unless I'm at the office, and I'm hoping that my normal, everyday clothes will be a little more appealing and less intimidating to her.

In case I make it to the office, I grab the hanger with a black dress shirt, black slacks and my silver tie.

As I leave my walk-in closet I sigh. "If only I had some answers," I say out loud to no one, and my skin vibrates, hard and hot. I stumble. "Ow." But just as quickly as it came on, it's gone. "This is getting ridiculous."

I march out of my room, irritated that I don't understand what is going on with me. I doubt it's something a doctor could help me with; I'm left to my own resources to try and figure this out.

I step into the kitchen to find Celeste, my housekeeper, is there. I hired Celeste about a year ago. She's a plump little thing, standing at about five feet tall. She has stark blonde hair – no doubt from a box – and baby blue eyes and is not at all unattractive. She's in her mid to late thirties and insists she loves her job. Despite my offer to let her live in one of my condos in this building, she doesn't. She'd rather live at her boyfriend's place.

"Good morning, Celeste."

"Good morning, sir. Breakfast?"

"Please. The usual."

"Coming right up," she says as she gets to work.

"I'll be in my office."

She nods and goes about my breakfast.

As I walk toward my office, I take a look around my condo, wondering idly if it is something Vivienne would enjoy or feel comfortable in.

The shades are open, and light is flooding into the dining and living rooms. The floor is a beautiful walnut hardwood with a dark, glossy finish. My walls are painted a neutral tan, and the furniture is an eclectic mix of modern sofas and high-backed chairs. It's quite stuffy and formal, if you want the truth of it. But I don't spend mountains of time in the living and dining rooms.

When I'm home, I'm usually in my office, working, my bedroom, sleeping, or my entertainment room, which from here is behind the kitchen.

I reach my office door at the far end of the long, rectangular living room, I turn back towards the kitchen again and there is a sudden image shift of a little girl making a figure eight on a big wheel. I smile at the thought and open the door.

The flooring changes from wood to black slate, an after-market modification to accompany the bleached white walls. My desk, to the right of the door, is contemporary: black with silver accents and white drawers. The drawers are out to the sides and the top of the desk only sits on the corner of the cabinets. The front is held up by a single leg, and the overall appearance is that it's floating.

When I wake up the computer, I find two emails from Jack. The first one lets me know they've tapped into some information and that he wants to meet with me later today once they have something a little more concrete. The next contains a single image. A photo taken by one of the Capella Towers security cameras last night at about two in the morning. In the image I can see Elton and a younger gentleman. "Hello, Riley."

I pick up the card Detective Stevens left when he was here last night and forward the image to his email address with the note, *Taken Friday morning around 2 a.m. outside of Capella Towers.*

"Here you are, sir." Celeste comes into my office carrying a tray.

"Thanks, Celeste."

She sets it down on the desk and departs.

I plow through my food and grab my jacket on the way out. I'm hoping to catch Vivienne leaving her apartment this morning on her way to the hospital for her appointment. My intention for being there is so that she can see me and know that I knew about her appointment. It will either irritate the crap out of her or warm her up to talking to me at the hospital. The only reason I'm going is to see her, and I don't care if she knows that or not.

Six

By the time I arrive at the corner of Lake Street and Chicago, my back is on fire once again. There is a cab parked right outside the entrance to her apartment. Good – maybe she called a cab to take her to the hospital. If not, she has about five minutes to catch the bus if she's going to make it to the hospital on time.

I park in my usual spot and watch. I look for the police cruiser Red told me about and see it parked less than a block away.

The bus that she should have been on comes and goes, and the cab remains. It's chilly out this morning; a plume of exhaust smoke billows out of the cab's tailpipe.

My phone rings. It's Jack.

"Blake."

"Hi, Mikah. Listen, I have something I need you to see."

"Like?"

"Well you dropped a couple of names on me last night. Rebecca Black for one. She was found dead Thursday morning by the dumpster of a motel near Vivienne's that's well-known for prostitution and drug use."

"Was she a drug addict?"

"We don't know that yet, but that's not what's important."

"What is?"

"The gentleman in the picture I sent you is Riley Bennett."

"I figured. I forwarded it to Detective Stevens this morning." I'm getting a little annoyed that he's not getting to the point. And why the hell hasn't Vivienne come out yet?

"We have video evidence that we need to submit to the police. We have a video of Riley Bennett dumping Rebecca Black's body. Then he appears to inject something into her arm. After he leaves the scene, she moves and twitches a bit, then falls still."

"Fuck!" I spat out. "Can we send it to Detective Stevens?"

"We're working on that. The source of the video is unclear. We're not sure if it's a legal recording. I have a couple of guys on their way over there to find out. If it is a legal recording, we will turn it over anonymously."

"Find out, and fast. I want this fucker to fry."

"On it, boss."

"Thanks. Anything else?" I ask.

"Not that can't wait until this afternoon. I will let you know if anything else comes up."

"Perfect, thanks."

"No problem." He hangs up.

I pull the detective's card from my pocket, dial the number and wait.

"Hhhello?"

The voice is tentative, groggy from sleep. Not like the confident officer I met last night. "Detective Stevens?" I ask.

He clears his throat. "Yes."

Much better. "This is Mikah Blake. We met last night."

"Oh, of course. What can I do for you?"

"I sent you an email this morning that shows your boy Riley meeting his dad outside my building around two this morning. I have a security detail working on the full video exchange."

"Are these cameras yours? The ones used to capture these images?"

"Yes, I had the security system installed a couple years ago, the previous one was shit." I can hear my own irritation coming through. "If we find something you can use, you call your evidence boys and have them come get it."

"Uh...that's great. Thank you." I can hear it in his voice: He's not used to being told how to do his job.

"Don't thank me yet. I want a report on Vivienne's building from last night."

"It doesn't work like that, Blake. This isn't *quid pro quo* here. What is your need to know?" The skepticism can be heard in his voice and the pain in my back spikes.

"Because when I arrived here this morning, there was a cab parked outside. Still is. I'd like to know when it arrived."

"I can't do that, Mr. Blake."

"Don't give me that bullshit. Why don't you call your guy parked down the block from her apartment and ask him. Then we can move on from there."

"Alright, hang on." There is a series of clicks. Then he comes back on the line. *Ring.* "Blake?"

"Yup." *Ring.* "Thanks, Detective." I know he's violating company policy. *Ring.* And, I know it's killing him to give in to my demands.

"Yeah." Irritation fills his voice. *Ring.* "Just don't say anything when he answers." *Ring.*

Click. "You've reached the voicemail of Officer Anders. Please leave—" *Click.*

"What the hell?" Stevens says. "It's ringing, so it's on. But why not answer?"

"Let's find out, shall we?"

Seven

I turn off the car, climb out and start walking across the street. I don't like the tingles radiating through my body. "When was he due to check in?"

"Once every two hours or so. Less if we're in an unmarked stakeout. So he would be checking—"

"Alright." I cross Lake Street and approach the cab. The driver is there, reading the paper. He jumps when I knock on the back window as I keep walking along the car. "What are you doing here?" I ask him.

He cracks the window a bit. "Waiting for a fare."

"Who?" I demand.

"What the fuck do you care?" he spats back.

"Just tell me who you're here for."

"It's none of your damn business." He rolls the window back up.

"Who is that?" Stevens asks in my ear.

"The cab driver of the cab outside the apartment. I'm almost to the squad car."

As I approach the squad car, I slow my pace. Nothing moves inside the car. "If this asshole is asleep, I'm going to have your department for lunch," I say into the phone.

31

I reach the car and rap loudly on the window. Nothing. Bending down, I look inside the car. Red. Bright, red fading to brown blood...

"Stevens, you have an officer down." I don't wait for his reply. I drop the phone and take off full tilt toward Vivienne's apartment.

Jesus, please, dear God, no. Not her. My back is ablaze, my body trembling with the buzzing I've been feeling for the last couple of weeks.

I beat on the cab's hood. "Call nine-one-one! NOW!" He nods.

I can hear sirens in the distance.

I grab the outer door, swinging it open so hard that the glass shatters. The next door is locked. I shoulder-check the glass — once, twice. Finally, on the third try, it gives way, and I go stumbling inside.

As I climb the stairs three and four at a time, I feel like I'm in a nightmare with never-ending hallways.

I reach the third floor and apartment nine. I pound on the door. "Vivienne!" Harder I pound and turn the knob, but it's locked. "Vivienne!" I ram my shoulder into the door, harder each time, and the door flies open. I storm into her apartment.

"Jesus! God! NO!" I shout.

I rush to the bed. Reaching up to her face, I pull the tape away from her mouth with one hand while I check for a pulse with the other. I can't feel one.

"No, damn it!" *Do not do this to me!*

There is blood everywhere, all over the sheets. It's still wet, but wherever she was hurt is no longer bleeding.

There is so much blood.

When I place one hand on top of the other and press into her chest to give her CPR, her sternum gives way more than it should, and I pull back immediately, afraid of causing more damage.

I lean down and place my cheek by her mouth, hoping and praying I will feel her breath against my skin.

Nothing.

Nothing...

Tears, tears – hot, molten tears stream down my cheeks – and the buzz, the buzz is gone.

Eight

Click...
Squeak...
Click...
Squeak...
Click, squeak. Click, squeak.
Click, squeak. Click, squeak.
White floors, white walls, white doors. No windows. Long, white hallway after long, white hallway.

Must...*buzz*...find...*buzz*... The zing is back, a mellow humming.

Finally I see the sign over the door at the end of the hall. The sign I've been seeking for at least the last ten minutes: *Chapel.*

I push hard on the doors, but they don't budge.
Breathe.
Breathe.
Damn it.
Reach for the handle.
Push handle downward.
Pull on handle.
The door opens.

All mechanical actions – no matter how seemingly simple, like breathing – have eluded me. *Breathe*, I tell myself over and over again.

I walk straight forward and collapse hard onto a rail that runs along the altar and I grip the upper part for support. My eyes drift upward, seeking the crucifix above the altar.

"Why? Why her?" Is all I can manage to sob.

Breathe.

I can't close my eyes. When I do, all I can see is her lifeless body strewn at awkward angles across her bed. Blood-soaked, pale, lifeless.

Breathe.

I know nothing about her. I do not know her from a woman I pass on the street. But my heart. My heart has been ripped from my chest.

Click. Steps. Heels. *Clang.*

"Mikah?" A woman's voice from behind me. A familiar voice. "Mikah. Mikah, look at me," she says.

I can't. I shake my head.

"Mikah, she's alive."

My head jerks up. I look her straight in the eye, unable to believe that I heard her correctly. Dr. Alston nods her head, as in answer to my unasked question.

Long, slow exhale. My head wobbles back, facing forward. *Thank you, God.* I feel a small sense of relief wash over me, quickly replaced by anxiety.

"She is in very bad shape, but she is alive. Mikah, look at me."

I slowly turn my head in her direction. My body is not my own. I feel disconnected. Seeing the expression on my face, she falters.

"Keep—" *Breathe.* "—talking," I finally manage to let out.

"She's in bad shape, Mikah. She lost a lot of blood. We've given her more than four pints."

Breathe.

"She has a skull fracture."

My breath hitches, and I stop breathing again.

"A serious concussion, swelling on her brain, a broken wrist, a dislocated shoulder..."

Start breathing, slowly.

"Six broken ribs and her right lung is partially collapsed. It's not going to be an easy road, Mikah."

"Bab—" I can't even finish the word. My breath has been stolen from my body.

She nods and takes a seat in a nearby pew behind me. I fall backwards off of the altar rail, landing awkwardly on my ass.

"Jesus, Mikah."

"Can— Bre—" I point at my mouth.

She gets up and rushes over to my side. "The baby is fine."

Sharp, loud inhale. "Fine?" What the fuck is going on with me? I can't wrap my head around why I'm having these reactions.

"For now, yes. We are far from out of the woods yet." She helps me to sit up. "I've set her arm and shoulder. I have to surgically repair one of her ribs and her lung. She is being prepped right now. I also have a neurosurgeon coming in to see if we can help reduce some of the pressure on her brain. All of this will be very taxing to her body, and I cannot make any promises. Do you understand me?"

I just nod.

"When you're ready, head up to surgery - the waiting room. I'll find you there when we're done. We will do everything we can to save both of them, Mikah. I promise you." She grips my shoulder as she stands. "I'll see you soon," she says as she leaves.

From farther back in the chapel she turns to me. "She's gained more than fifteen pounds since I've seen her last. Her weight gain may have just saved her life."

I want to smile, but I can't. "Thank you," I say very slowly.

"You're welcome."

She turns and leaves. I'm no longer having to force myself to breathe. She is alive. She's survived.

"Jesus, God, thank you."

I pull myself up off the floor and take a seat in the front pew, leaning my elbows into my knees.

I feel a vibration along my thigh. My phone. That is about the fifteenth time in the last half hour it's gone off, but frankly, I could care less right now.

Resting my head in my hands, I let the tears flow. They pool into my palms. Breathing deep, ragged breaths, I try to pull myself back together.

I need to go upstairs, but I can't go in the state I'm in. I don't understand why I'm having such a strong reaction to the news about Vivienne. Something I can't explain is happening to me. I need to see her.

"You will see her soon enough."

My head snaps up at the elegant, soft female voice. Nothing. I see no one.

"You've been chosen to protect her, Mikah. Chosen to see to it that she is safe."

I stand quickly, spinning around. Sharp, blinding pain bounces around my body, and I crumple to my knees.

"What— What is happening to me?" I say aloud.

No response. I ball my fists in frustration, and the pain stops as quickly as it started.

I climb back up into the pew, shaking now because it's not just the pain that's gone but the hum, too. My connection to Vivienne, and it's gone. Panic seeps in.

"Relax."

Relief washes through me in instant response to the command. I have no control over it.

"Why can't you tell me what is going on?"

"Your answers will come in time, when you're meant to hear them."

I feel like I'm losing my mind. I'm hearing voices, talking to myself. Yet I can feel someone with me.

"I am not for you to look upon, young angel. I am here to guide you, to help you into your new life. She is ours to protect, and we will. Without fail, we will protect her in the way she is meant to be protected. But we can only initiate the healing; she must do the rest on her own. When the time comes, you will be told what to do next."

"She doesn't want me around," I whisper.

"You do not need to speak aloud, young angel. I know what you think, and I feel what you feel. I believe that her life has taken the turn you need to keep her within reach. Do not fret."

I sigh. With the heels of my hands, I press against my temples, trying to dispel the idea that someone is talking to me inside my head. I'm not crazy, am I?

A sweet female giggle radiates through my whole body. The tingling is back, but this time it feels different; it tickles. I squirm. Then suddenly the sensation becomes a spreading warmth that comforts me.

I realize that, for the first time, I can interpret the sensations. The tickling is something happy. Or laughter? The warmth feels like love or adoration.

The sensation stops.

Hello?

There is no answer, but a warm calm spreads across my skin. I decide that staying down here in the chapel is only going to drive me nuts, so I head for the door.

I pull my phone from my pocket. Thirty-seven missed calls. I'm not at all interested in any of them. Most of them are from Jack. But one...

I open up the visual voicemail app.

Elton Bennett
09:57 32 seconds
"What kind of game are you playing at, Blake? How dare you pull of out of our arrangement. You will not get away with this. She's just a white trash tramp who needed to be dealt with. Don't go getting too hasty, you will burn for it. I'll see to it."

I click into my voicemail, find the message from Bennett and forward it to Stevens.

"A little tramp, huh? What are *you* playing at, Bennett?" I say as I reach the door to the chapel.

It doesn't surprise me that he's found a connection; he's a crooked-ass, wannabe politician. It's clear to me that his attempts to cover his own ass are backfiring already.

Nine

I leave the chapel and head down the hall towards toward the bank of elevators that will take me up to the surgery floor. I'd rather wait up there then down here.

Jesus, what the hell was all that about? I shake my head but can't dispel the image of an angel – the painting my mom had above the hutch – from my mind. Could all that talk, all those years ago, really be true? Am I really an angel? But if I'm an angel, doesn't that mean that I died?

"Not necessarily."

"Jesus!" I sputter, stumbling in my surprise. Falling against the wall, I look behind me, but there's no one there. There's not a person to be seen in either direction.

"No, not Jesus, angel. I am Seraphina – your guardian, your teacher."

Rather than look like an idiot talking to myself in the middle of a deserted hallway, I try speaking to her in my thoughts. *Then show yourself.*

Good God, I really am loosing it.

"I cannot show myself to you. Not until you're ready."

But don't you think it will help me better understand what is going on?

"Not hardly, young angel. You have a lot to learn. When you're ready, you will see."

The more she talks, the more convinced I am that she's not the same voice that spoke to me in the chapel. Ugh! I don't know how much of this I'm supposed to handle before I break.

Does this have anything to do with the tattoo on my back?

"Everything. Although, young one, it is not a tattoo."

I nod my head. *I'm growing well aware of that. I swear I saw it shimmering last night. What on earth is it?*

"Why, what else would an angel have upon his back?"

My knees buckle as reality strikes. *Wings?*

The answer to my question comes in the form of a tingling sensation radiating across my back. The reinforcement of my conclusion leaves me shaking my head. This is all just way too much. *Are you going to keep blindsiding me when you start talking?*

"Yes, and no. Now, young angel, know that I will be ever-present and will do my best not to frighten you."

I push away from the wall and begin moving back down the hall. Finally I reach the elevator and press the up arrow.

There are so many unanswered questions, I feel like my head is going to explode. But something that the other voice told me comes flooding back.

The voice before, she said something about helping Vivienne. What did she mean?

"She meant that we can only help her start the process. The rest is up to her. You are here to protect her, to keep her safe and to help her heal."

How on earth am I supposed to do that?

"Be here."

Well that won't be hard., I have no intention of leaving. Not until she does.

The elevator finally arrives and I step in. As the elevator rises, all the angst and anguish I felt earlier returns. I get this strange sense of emptiness, and I wonder if the voice has gone.

When I get no answering reply, I'm assured that she is. At least for now. With each passing floor, my anxiety rises, and the buzz strengthens across my skin. But for the first time in all of this, I feel a sense of hope.

Ten

I've never been a fan of hospitals, let alone waiting rooms. The last time I spent any amount of time in one was after the accident. My youngest brother, Ronin, had survived the initial accident, then surgery, only to pass away about six hours later. We waited, Victoria and I, for nearly four hours while he was in surgery. We had already found out about Dad and my other brother, Shane.

I spent hours pacing the room while Victoria slowly lost her mind. She was far closer to Dad and Ronin than I ever was. I had always been closer to Mom.

All things considered, I will take this waiting room over that one, only because I feel completely confident in Dr. Alston's abilities as well as my newfound sense of hope.

Though that doesn't stop me from pacing the room, thankful that I'm the only one in here.

My phone starts to vibrate. Hoping that it will offer some distraction, I pull it from my pocket. My eyebrows knit together.

"Blake."

"Mikah, it's Detective Stevens."

"Have you caught Riley yet?"

"No." So not the distraction I was looking for. "I called because I received your recording. How in the hell did you obtain this?"

"It's a simple voicemail recording. Leaving a voicemail is public record."

I can hear a heavy sigh on the other end of the phone. "I see your point. How is she?"

My eyes water almost instantly at his seemingly innocent question, but his sense of guilt is palpable even through the phone. "She's in surgery, so I don't know."

"Alright. I'll try back later."

"Detective?"

Another sigh. "Yeah," he says, clipped.

"How are you holding up?" I ask. Doubtless, his dead officer weighs heavy on his mind.

"Officer Anders was a good friend of mine. I'm..." Pause.

"No need, Detective. I understand."

"Thanks, Blake."

"Yup. When my people get in touch with you, let me know if you need anything from them. Or from me."

"Will do. Thanks."

"Anytime." I hear the disconnecting click.

I pull the phone from my ear and hit end. I take a step back when I see more of the missed calls. My leg bumps into a chair, so I sit down and begin scrolling through them.

Most of them are from Jack, and looking at the time on my watch and the call log tells me that the majority of them were from before Elton left his message. It's good to know that, had I been coherent and not hearing voices in my head, I would've had a heads-up about what he knew before calling me.

I go flipping through the emails. I quickly see why Elton knows about my severing ties to Bennett and Lisbon, which means pulling out of the condo project we broke ground on a couple weeks ago. Elton knows that he cannot continue without MSBE's involvement. Ninety percent of the investors on that project only joined in because I was fronting the majority of it. The project was a major risk, given its location.

Jack has also forwarded some more information regarding Riley and his involvement in Rebecca's death.

I can't look at this now. I don't need to have what could've happened to Vivienne shoved in my face.

Jesus. Vivienne. She was done, gone, out of Riley's life, and by the sounds of it, never to return. She could've had anything she wanted out of Elton. Or Riley, for that matter. She could've used them, blackmailed them, anything. But she didn't. Why?

I know why. She's not that type of person. Her determination to be independent through all of this is my answer. Whether it is to prove it to herself or not, she's determined to make it on her own.

Eleven

A hum radiates quickly through my body as the sound of footsteps registers in my ears. This time it's light, but doesn't tickle. Someone that I know is coming?

After four more steps, a man steps into the doorway. My heart races for that brief second before recognition, and then the humming stops.

"Red. What are you doing here?"

"I came by to check on you."

"How'd you know I was—…"

"You would think, after the last three years, you would know the answer to that question."

I nod my head. "She's in surgery."

"I feel awful about this."

I look to him, puzzled. "For?"

"I was there. Last night. Waiting for her to return home from work. If I'd gotten there sooner I—…"

"Stop. There was a cop who was killed in Riley's quest to get to her. Do not think that it would have been any different with you had you arrived earlier." I lean forward, resting my elbows on my knees, and look down at the floor. "The truth is that I don't know when the cop was killed. Riley could have been in that building for hours before she got home. Or he could have managed to sneak his way in, leaving the cop for later. Something that surprised me most was the fact that her door was locked, but only the knob." I wonder idly if Riley had left, met with his father outside of my building and then went back.

The buzz comes back, same as a moment ago, as I hear Red's shoes hit the carpet.

He sits down next to me. "I know, but still, it makes me wonder." He stops talking and I can sense his mood change to distress. "Good Lord, Mikah, you're bleeding."

I give Red a sideways glance as I try and recall how I could have started bleeding. He's looking at my back. Shit! "Where?" I ask, a little bit of panic in my voice. I can't feel any pain anywhere.

"There, on your shoulder and your back. Let me look at it."

"No, it's fine it's probably not my blood,." I say, as my body runs cold and as the vision of Vivienne splayed out on that bed, blood everywhere, goes flashing through my mind.

"Jesus, Mikah, you're white as a ghost." I try - and fail - to dispel the image from my mind, so I open my eyes, attempting to give myself something else to look at.

Red is quick to distract me. "You alright *mo chara*?"

My lips turn up slightly at his use of Irish and English together. "I think so." Is all I can manage to say at this point.

"I have some jeans and a t-shirt for you in the car if you'd like?" Red asks. I just nod. "Alright, I'll be right back. Anything else?"

"Coffee would be great. Thanks." I look up at him. There is pity on his face, and though the look doesn't bother me, I can understand now why Vivienne would see that look and hate it.

"Sure thing." He turns and walks out of the room.

Looking through the glass at the nurse's station reveals that nothing has changed. Though I can't see everything, I can see that line number four, Vivienne's line, still says she's in surgery with Dr. Alston.

Despair washes over me in a rush. Come on, damn it. Something. Anything.

Twelve

A few minutes later, Red returns with a bag containing a pair of jeans, a gray t-shirt and my sneakers.

"Will you stay here? Wait until I get back?"

"Of course, sir," he says with a smile.

I give him a half-hearted lift of the corner of my mouth and head toward the desk.

"We haven't heard anything yet, Mr. Blake," says the young blond nurse behind the desk.

"I figured as much. But I need to change my clothes. Is there a restroom I can change in?"

"Not really, but room three—" she points to her left and down the hall "—is empty. Feel free to use it to change and freshen up."

"Thanks," I say.

As I pass the whiteboard, I glance just to make sure that nothing has changed. Nope. Still says *Callahan, OR 4, general/personal, Alston, 2 hrs.*

So much for two hours; it's been nearly three.

I pick up my pace, wanting to be back in the waiting room when Dr. Alston comes out.

Room three is obviously a recovery room: There's no bed, but there are several machines that appear to be turned off. I can't help but notice the ultrasound machine in the corner opposite everything else. The room smells like bleach and sanitizer. Fresh. I silently hope this is not where she will go when she's out of surgery. She deserves better than this room.

I shake my head and get to work unbuttoning my shirt and pants and kicking off my shoes. Opening the bag reveals a stash of toiletries – shampoo, conditioner, shave gel, a razor, two combs, cologne and deodorant – and I smile a little at Red's foresight.

Once I'm down to my undershirt, boxer briefs and socks I head for the bathroom.

I take stock in the mirror. There are dark red to brown spots of varying sizes on the shoulder of my undershirt. It is also ripped in several places. My other shirt wasn't like this, was it? No doubt Red would have thrown a bigger fit about my being looked at had my shirt been ripped.

I turn around to pick it up to check, but before I can complete my turn, something on my back catches my eye. I turn my back to the mirror and look over my shoulder, and the emptiness I felt earlier disappears completely, replaced by the sense that someone is with me.

"Do not fret. You have done well, young angel. You knew I was here." It's the same voice as in the hallway.

"What is all over my back?" I stare blankly at the silver-gray tint to the back of my already gray shirt.

"Ah, young angel, it has begun."

"What, damn it? What is going on?" I nearly shout, and then quickly silence myself, hoping no one heard my outburst.

"Calm, Mikah. Remove your shirt and you shall see."

I reach for the hem and turn my head back toward the room before pulling my shirt over my head. I take a deep breath as the voice starts to sing.

Is the singing really necessary?

She laughs. "No, young one, it is not, but I am bored."

"Seriously?" I say out loud. "I'm on the verge of a damn freak-out and you're bored. Brilliant."

She laughs again. "Mikah, you will quickly see that I am bored constantly. You, young angel, are alive. Blood courses through your veins, your heart beats. But I, I am left here in whiteness for eternity. Yes, I get bored – very easily, mind you – and the only time I get to have any amount of fun at all is when I am in your head."

I shiver at the thought of this voice having a good time in my head. "How long have you been in my head without me knowing?" She laughs again. "This really isn't funny, Seraphina."

"You are right, Mikah. Getting your wings is serious business."

"My what?" I'm thrown. Wings? Real wings? "How am I supposed to go walking around with wings on my back?"

"Now we're getting somewhere." I feel an attitude shift in my head, almost like excitement. "Go ahead, take a look in the mirror. You will see."

I begin to turn my head and the excitement bubbles. But it's not my excitement.

Seriously?

"Oh, come on. This is fun," she says, and now I can hear the excitement in her voice.

I try to shake her excitement off and turn my head a little bit more. I don't know what to expect, and I'm freaking out about what I'm going to see. *Good grief, stop being such a baby.*

"I agree."

"Would you stop that?"

She giggles. Out of all the angels in...wherever she is...I get stuck with the damn comedian.

"Hmph," she huffs.

Finally, I continue turning my head until I'm able to see my back.

Thirteen

There on my back, in vivid detail, are two beautiful wings with white, gray, and silver feathers. They are nothing but a flat, two-dimensional image, yet they seem to be alive.

My knees give out and I tumble to the floor, breathing heavily.

She is quiet for a few moments while this all soaks in. "The legend is true, an angel are you," she finally says.

I'm unable to speak aloud. *You can say that again. But me? Why me?*

"Because, young angel, it is who you are. It is who your mother was and is to this day; though she never grew wings while she was alive, she is one of us now."

Can I see her?

"Perhaps in time. She is one of our *máithreacha*, who are very busy."

Máithreacha*? Mothers?*

"Yes. They are second in command to our *máthair go léir*. Your mother was the one who spoke to you first and, as you no doubt guessed, she can be a bit testy."

How did I not recognize her voice? It's a voice that plays in my head constantly whenever I do something profoundly stupid.

"If you think about that long enough, I'm sure you can figure that out."

Suddenly I understand: She didn't want me to know it was her.

"Or perhaps you didn't recognize her because you were not thinking of her that way."

I think back to the voice in the chapel. I still can't hear it as my mother's, but I take Seraphina's word for it.

Anxiety washes over me as I contemplate the responsibilities that might come with these wings. *What happens now?*

"We wait until the right time and place for you to take control of them. Then you can learn to use them to your advantage."

I let out a rushed breath, thanking the stars that I can deal with this later. Given that there was blood on my shirt but no pain, I'm not quite convinced that I'm not dreaming.

In the instant that thought crosses my mind, sharp, white-hot pain races around my body, and I fall flat on my back.

Alright I get it; I'm not dreaming!

The pain stops, and I regain control of my own body and senses. I stand up and look into the mirror, this time facing forward. Where the blood had soaked into my t-shirt on my shoulder and chest, there is...nothing. Absolutely nothing there.

"You're a fast healer, young angel."

"The door at her apartment. The one I shattered with my shoulder. It caused all that blood, but where...where are the cuts?" I whisper.

"As I said, you are a fast healer."

"I... What? Jesus. Is there anything else you want to tell me about before I discover it for myself and go ballistic?"

"You've already had enough for today. Get dressed and go back to the waiting room. I will do what I can to leave you alone for the rest of the day."

I nod, and once again the emptiness returns. The hum in my back disappears. I flex my shoulder, testing its strength, but it feels fine. Completely normal. Which ranks up there with talking to angels in my head in my list of strange things that have happened to me today.

Fourteen

As I walk past the nurse's station, I glance at the board and it's changed: Vivienne's name is no longer listed on the forth line. I jog back to the waiting room.

Stepping into the room, I notice Red in the corner, reading a magazine, and a family sitting opposite him. I walk straight up to him. He puts down his magazine.

"Has Dr. Alston been here yet?"

"No, but the nurse came in and said that she was out of surgery and the doctor would be in as soon as she could."

I let out a rush of breath as a weight lifts from my shoulders. She's out of surgery. "Oh, thank stars."

He chuckles a bit at my expression, something he does all the time. I explained to him once why I have a hard time thanking God or some other higher power for the things that happen to people. After you've lost your mother, your father and your two brothers and you have a sister that is lost inside her own head, it's hard to be thankful for the things that God does.

I take a seat, though I know it's going to be pointless; I'm beyond keyed up, and I feel like pacing again. But I don't want to freak out the family sitting across from us.

What a damn mess today has turned into. First Vivienne, and then angels start talking to me in my head. Now my back. How in the hell does this stuff happen to me? Why me? I cannot seem to find a reason for it. I grew up believing that to become an angel you had to die first, be pure of self, and follow a spiritual path. All of these things I'm not.

Wings? Really? How on earth am I supposed to hide these things? What in the world is going to happen to me – physically and mentally?

I've only been sitting here for a few minutes when the skin on my back starts to crawl. I shiver and grab the back of my neck, massaging it, hoping that the contact will lessen the sensation. But instead, a strong sense of unease comes over me. I feel restless. I need to move, be doing something – anything but sitting here idle and waiting. But I can't make myself move.

"Err, you alright, lad?"

I turn to look at Red. His eyes flare momentarily and there is an instance of unease that bounces off of him. Jesus.

"What's wrong?"

"Your eyes, they're..." he pauses, and instinctively I shut them tight. "They're almost black." Shit.

Seraphina, damn it, where are you?

"I don't know," I answer him.

In the next instant, my body tenses and I feel a warmth radiate through my body and dissipate instantly. "I'll be right back." I get up and start for the door and the hallway. I walk past the nurse's station, back to the room I just came from, and quickly lock the door behind me. I head straight to the bathroom mirror.

I shudder at the sight of nearly black eyes.

"Oh dear." I hear Seraphina's voice.

"What in the world is going on?" I say out loud.

"You're in the hospital."

"Yeesss..." I say, trying hard not to be sarcastic with her.

"Is your skin crawling?"

I just nod, not able to answer because I can't stop staring at the solid black of my eyes.

"Someone near you, not known to you, has died."

My heart sinks momentarily. "So why am I reacting this way?"

"Because the person who has died has been taken by evil."

I feel a tightness in my shoulders that pushes outward.

"Oh, no, you don't. Not here. You'll rip your shirt."

"What?" I say sharply and turn quickly. In the mirror I can see two rather sharp, knobby points beneath my shirt, up near the tops of my shoulders. Right...where...

Fifteen

I feel my head start to spin. Seraphina begins to chant in a tongue I do not recognize. An ache spreads across my back, and I can feel my shirt shift as it settles back against my skin.

I brace myself against the sink, my stomach rolling. I feel like retching.

"Eventually, young angel, you will be able to control this yourself. I've put your angel soul to rest. It won't last forever, but it will be enough to allow you to calm down."

Thank you.

I'm so confused. All of this is just...it's too much. The wings, the changes – it's all so overwhelming. I haven't even begun to process it all, and I feel like my life is no longer my own.

"I understand that this is difficult for you."

Gah! Stop that. It's hard to think when you're in there listening to everything I think.

She laughs. "Yes, it can be a bit obnoxious, but it is also something to take comfort in. I am here to guide and teach you."

I know, but it's hard. I know the story and I know the poem, but I feel like I'm missing something. I feel like I need my head examined.

"Believe me, young one, when the time is right, you will know. When you accept your destiny, you will be taught all you need to know."

How will I know when I'm ready?

"When your mind is free. Now go. Your young lady needs you."

The emptiness returns, and I shiver. How am I supposed to accept this?

I slowly turn around to face the mirror, hoping that what she has said is right. I slowly open my eyes. Back to blue and green. I let out a rushed breath.

Now how on earth do I explain this to Red?

I walk slowly back down the hall toward the waiting room. Anxiety knots my stomach, but – I suddenly realize – the buzz in my back is gone. I flex my shoulders. My back is no longer tight, but loose and normal. Weird.

In the waiting room, Red is still in his same chair, reading the same magazine. I take my seat next to him.

"Feel better?" he asks as he puts down the magazine.

"Much," I say back.

He doesn't press for more information. I gather that he has been around me long enough to not ask questions.

"You can take off," I tell him.

"I'd like to stay. Make sure you're alright."

I shrug my shoulders. "Alright."

I notice that we are alone once again in the waiting room and outside the door there are several nurses gathered around the desk. Looking beyond them to the board, I see that the majority of the rooms are now empty.

"What is taking so long?" I ask aloud, not expecting an answer.

"The nurse came in about three minutes ago, said Dr. Alston was on her way."

"Finally."

I sit back and pull my ankle up onto my knee. I put my head back against the wall behind me and close my eyes.

And instead of seeing the black of my eyelids, my vision shifts...

Sixteen

The image is white but three-dimensional, almost like a room. Yes, now I can make out a couch and table in front of me, but they too are as white as the walls and the floor. I can see something in the distance – not white, but dressed in white – coming closer to me. My heart rate speeds up, not in fear but in anticipation. Whatever is coming toward me is something I want, something I need. But what?

I watch as the figure draws closer. I feel myself growing restless with excitement. It seems to be taking forever, and I want to walk toward the figure, but I can't. I'm frozen in place.

The figure draws nearer still, and finally I'm beginning to make out who is walking toward me. The bright red, curly, flowing hair belongs to Vivienne.

"Mikah." It's not the voice I was expecting, not Vivienne's voice. "Mikah." It's Red. I feel his arm nudge mine. My eyes fly open. "Dr. Alston's coming."

"What?" Shit. I rub my eyes, hoping to dispel the image, but as soon as my eyes close again, I see her. She hasn't moved.

I open my eyes again to the drab carpet of the waiting room, blink a few times and stand up. "How long was I out?" I ask Red.

"About three minutes."

"Well shit. I feel like I was out for hours." That is an understatement. Red just laughs.

"Nah, you're alright," he says.

I turn my head to look out the door. Dr. Alston is standing at the nurse's desk. It looks as though she's signing something. I start walking toward the door, but she holds her palm up toward me, gesturing for me to stop, then quickly puts up one finger.

Gah! Doesn't she know this is killing me?

Seventeen

I start to pace: toward Red, back toward the door, and back toward Red again. Come on, damn it. This is killing—

"Mikah."

My head snaps up and I turn around to face the tall, leggy blond. Dr. Alston. Under different circumstances I might have found her attractive. In fact, at some point I probably did. But that was before I met Vivienne.

"What's taken so long?" I ask her sharply. Too sharply. "Sorry."

"It's alright, I know you're anxious." I nod. "It's taken so long because we needed to do a post-op CAT scan. I wanted to have those results before I came to talk to you."

"And those are what, exactly?"

"I'll get there. First, she is out of surgery. The next twenty-four hours are critical, so we have her in a medically induced coma."

I feel my eyes flare. I'm instantly worried about what happened earlier. I take quick stock of my body, but nothing has changed.

"We were able to repair her shattered rib and her lung, but she has some significant swelling in her brain and we weren't able to do anything to relieve the pressure. However, the post-op CAT scan showed some improvement since the first one we did. Which is a good sign. Keeping her sedated will mean better chances for a faster recovery. We will do another scan tomorrow morning to see how the swelling is doing. If it has gone down some more, we may be able to gauge how much longer we'll need to keep her in a coma until the swelling is gone completely."

I'm forcing each breath in and out of my body as she is telling me this, trying desperately to soak it all in. "Can I see her?" I ask shakily.

"Yes."

I start to move toward the door.

"I'm not done."

I stop and turn back to her.

"She is being moved to a private room upstairs. A cot is being brought in. I'm assuming you will refuse to leave her until she's awake?" I nod. "Okay, so let them get her moved and settled."

"What about the baby?" I say, breathless.

"Relax, Mikah. As I said, the next twenty-four hours are critical. We won't know anything definite for a couple of days, but I can tell you that there is a very strong heartbeat and we are monitoring for any distress."

It just became a little easier to breathe. I've yet to figure out why I have such an attachment to this baby, but I do.

"Anything else?" I ask.

"Medically, no, not right now. Other than she has a broken wrist and her shoulder has been set. It is in a sling and strapped across her body to prevent any movement. It is also acting as double duty for her ribs."

I remember her telling me this before, but it still strikes me dumb at the brutality. I haven't even wanted to imagine what he did besides cut and beat her, but I guess my face betrays the unasked question.

"She wasn't raped." I fall into the nearest chair. "Judging by the severe bruising on her ankles and wrists, and by those around her neck, I imagine that was the intention, but we've checked her for any internal damage and there are no recent signs."

My head falls into my hands. "Jesus Christ, what has she been through?"

"As a medical professional, I can't tell you that. The only reason I'm telling you this much is because I know that her next of kin is her mother, who isn't of sound mind, and..." She pauses. I look at her to continue. "When she was here last time, when you brought her in." I nod. "She listed you as her emergency contact on the paperwork I left for her. Amanda, my nurse, found it in her room after she was discharged."

My heart skips a few beats, and I know I stop breathing. I have no clue why something as inconsequential as leaving my name as a point of contact has such a profound effect on me. Hell, I don't know much of anything anymore.

"She's broken, Mikah, and as much as I know you want to fix her, you need to talk to her first. Get to know her. Her physical history is telling. I have no doubt that if approached in the right fashion, she will open up and start talking to you. But don't push her," she says with a glare. I nod my understanding. "She's upstairs, top floor."

Immediately I stand and hold out my hand. She takes it. "Thank you," I say sincerely as I fight back the tears that threaten to spill over.

"My pleasure. Go. See her, be with her. I warn you though – she has a tube in her mouth, a machine is breathing for her, and she is very badly bruised up. And that is only what is starting to show now. So be ginger with her."

I nod solemnly and head for the door and the elevator to my right. As I push the up button, I sense Red approaching.

"Go home, *cara*. No need for you to be here," I say at the same time that he pushes the down button.

"I know."

"Thank you. I really appreciate you being here."

"I know. I'll be back around six with food. Here, take this." He hands me the duffle bag with my stuff in it. I take it from him. "Your chargers are in there, plus your laptop. Need anything else from home?"

I hear the ding of the elevator to my right and head toward it. "Right now, no. I will call if I think of something."

He nods as the doors slide open and I step in.

"Oh, call Detective Stevens for me. Tell him what Dr. Alston said and that if he needs me, he knows where to find me."

"Got it," he says as the doors close.

Eighteen

As I come around the corner from the elevator, I see two cops standing outside of a room. Neither is talking to the other, which I find strangely comforting. At least I know they're paying attention. The one closest to me turns in my direction as I approach.

"How can we help you?" he says.

"I'm Mikah Blake. I'm here to see Vivienne Callahan."

He nods in recognition of my name but turns to face me, feet apart, at the ready.

"I need to see some identification, please."

I'm not sure whether to be irritated or impressed by his question. I reach for my wallet, but it's not there. Damn it.

"It's in my bag," I say, letting him know that I need to reach into someplace he can't see.

"Mind if I check?" he asks.

I hold out the bag to him.

"Set it down, please, and take three steps back."

I seriously want to roll my eyes. I'm the last person they need to worry about. But I take a comfort in knowing that if I have to go through this much trouble, so will everyone else.

I take the three steps back plus one for good measure, trying not to seem as impatient as I feel. "It should be right on top," I say. "If it's not there, then it's in the long side pocket."

He begins opening up the zipper on the top. I can see when he opens it that my wallet is not there. My heart skips a beat. Crap, I could have sworn I put it in the main compartment.

He doesn't hesitate but goes straight into the side pocket. I can't see what he's seeing, but he puts his hand in and moves a few things around. "Is this it?" He looks up at me as he pulls out my black leather wallet.

"Yes, sir."

He stands back up, looking inside the wallet, glancing from me to the driver's license. "I need to search your bag, Mr. Blake."

"Whatever you need."

He bends back down and starts glancing through my bag. Nothing but a few articles of clothing and my shaving kit are inside. Laptop and cell phone chargers are also in there, but he seems satisfied at a cursory glance.

"Can you put your hands on the wall next to you?"

Oh for crying out loud. I turn toward the wall, put my hands up and spread my legs slightly. He comes up behind me and quickly pats down my under my arms and hips and runs his hands down the outside of my legs to my ankles and stands.

"Here's your wallet. As long as were here, we won't bother you again. Our shift changes at midnight. After that, make sure you have at least your wallet when you leave the room," he states matter-of-factly.

"How long will officers be posted here?" I ask.

"Until she is discharged or the suspect is caught, whichever comes first."

"Detective Stevens?"

He nods curtly. "He's pretty adamant about keeping her well-protected. From what I understand of the situation, I don't blame him for that."

I nod at him. "May I go in now?"

"Absolutely." He steps aside, and the other officer moves away from the door to allow me to pass.

I can't help but feel slightly grateful for their presence here. "Thank you, gentlemen," I say.

After all my eagerness to see her, I suddenly feel anxious.

As if in slow motion, I watch my hand reach for the door handle. Turn it. I hear and feel the click as it unlatches. I push, moving forward with the door. It feels like minutes before I clear the jamb and step into the room.

A curtain separates me from the rest of the room. I shut the door behind me. Soft lamp light comes through the curtain.

It takes a moment before I can make myself step past the curtain; after everything Dr. Alston told me about her condition, I'm afraid of what I'm going to see on the other side. Then the image of her walking toward me in the dream surfaces – Vivienne in a white gown, her vibrant red hair flowing over her shoulders. Beautiful.

I take a deep breath, reach for the curtain with my free hand and gingerly slide it back. I let out the breath I've been holding when I realize that I can't really see anything yet. There is a small hallway and the room opens up to the left.

I set my bag down along the wall opposite the bathroom and take a few steps forward. The room is decorated in pale blues with a flower wallpaper boarder at the top of the walls. The only furniture is a cherry wood cabinet, a roll-away bed with blankets and pillows on top, and Vivienne's bed.

As I take another step into the room, I hear the faint, rhythmic wheezing of pressurized air being forced through a tube, then sucked out again. In and out.

Suck it up, buttercup, I tell myself and take that last step to bring me around the corner of the short hallway so I can get a full view of the bed and Vivienne.

Nineteen

The bed is laid out flat, but she is turned slightly away from me. It only takes me a moment to realize it's because there's a pillow underneath her shoulder and arm, which allows her arm to rest on the pillow rather than being held by a sling.

Her gorgeous red hair is splayed out across the top of the bed, and I can see the tube going into her mouth. Her eyes are closed. Her face looks peaceful, relaxed.

She actually looks quite comfortable.

On closer inspection, I see the bruising around her neck that Dr. Alston was talking about, and my heart stutters. I see where they put the IV into her left arm, and further down, the deep purple bruising around her wrist. I just want to cry, an urge further aggravated by the constant pushing and pulling of air through the machine.

A small movement next to the bed catches my eye. Coming from a machine, below a monitor, is a long, narrow strip of paper that has piled up and curled around on itself. It looks like calculator tape. My eyes pop up to the machine it's coming from. A heart monitor line bounces quickly across the screen with the number one hundred fifty above it. To the right of the one hundred fifty is the name *Baby Callahan*.

The baby's heart rate is so fast. Is that normal? I have no idea. I remember it was fast before, but I didn't realize it would be that fast.

My eyes follow four thick black wires that disappear under the covers. On the other side of the bed from the fetal monitor are the IV machine, monitors for Vivienne, and a brown leather chair.

I walk around the bed and sit down. It's only about four thirty, but I'm exhausted. All the adrenaline of the day is more than my body can handle. Looking at Vivienne makes me ashamed of my own tiredness; she's been through far more today than I have.

God she looks so pale, fragile. She always looked fragile, but right now she looks so vulnerable to everything. But she has survived all this; I can never think of her as weak and vulnerable ever again. She is strong, and this woman has an amazing determination to survive. Compared to all I imagine she's been through, living through the deaths of my family members is nothing.

I lean forward and place my forehead on the bed railing. "Vivienne, I'm so sorry," I say. "I wish I'd gotten there faster. Or that I'd never let you go back to that apartment in the first place."

Beep, beep, beep.

The sound is coming from my right. I look up at the heart monitor, which shows a flat line sliding to the left of the screen followed by the up and downs of her heartbeat. Above the normal monitor line is an image. It is the same as what is scrolling along the bottom, except in the place of where there should have been two of her regular heartbeats, there is nothing but a flat line.

"Vivienne?"

A slow beat, then silence.

"Vivienne, can you hear me?"

Another slow beat.

"Vivienne, I'm here. I'm so, so sorry."

Silence.

My heart races, then the machine blips again and the heartbeat comes back strong. I can't help but smile. She knows I'm here. Whether it is a conscious thought or not, she knows.

I blink back the tears. I want to touch her, but I'm afraid to. It looks like everywhere hurts. I decide against it for now. But I do lower the bed rail so that it's not separating us, pull the chair closer to the bed, and put my head gently on the mattress near her shoulder. "I'm here, I won't leave." And I let my eyes slowly close.

Twenty

It doesn't take but a moment for the vision to return. A different white room this time; this one has two windows. But the scenery beyond them is little more than a white blur. Taking a moment to look around, I see that some other things have changed. There is a white vase on the white coffee table, filled with white flowers.

The only color is Vivienne's red, flowing hair as she continues to walk toward me. This time she is moving faster, but she's still so far away. I try once again to walk toward her but I can't; I'm rooted to the floor by some invisible force.

I watch as she comes closer and becomes clearer, more defined. I can make out some of the silver accents on her dress. Intricate designs on the white material. The dress is a plunging v-neck with a silver belt below her breasts. It flows out behind her as she walks. She looks beautiful with a white flower over her left ear. She smiles at me and my heart melts. I want to hold her so bad.

I put out my arms and notice that they are bare and more muscular than in real life. And there's an intricate tribal tattoo running along my right arm. Where the hell did that come from? I look down at my body and see first that I'm shirtless and then that the tattoo continues onto my chest. I am wearing pants, thank God. White ones that almost look like pajamas.

I look back up at Vivienne. She's gotten a lot closer, but she is still a ways off. I flex my shoulders in impatience, and that's when I hear and feel it at the same time: a shifting on my back. I flex again, and Vivienne giggles.

My heads snaps up in her direction. She is covering her mouth with her hand in an attempt to stifle her laugh. I want to ask her what she is laughing at when I feel the movement again.

My stomach sinks. I'm not sure I'm ready for this, but I turn my head slowly to the right. I'm met with a wall of white feathers.

Instinctively I turn to better see it, but as I move, so does the wall of feathers. Damn it.

She laughs again.

"This is not funny," I say out loud.

She laughs again anyway.

I turn again, and still it moves with me. With my left hand I reach out, trying to grab it, to touch it. The moment my hand makes contact with the feathers, pure, undiluted pleasure courses through my body and I feel my knees buckle. I quickly pull my hand away and look back toward Vivienne.

She is pointing to my left so I turn in that direction. A mirror. How did I miss this before?

I look back at Vivienne. She points again, with more urgency, so I take a step toward the mirror. And another.

Shapes and colors begin to coalesce in the mirror with each passing step. I close my eyes, afraid of what I might see, and take three more steps.

"Mr. Blake."

I can't open my eyes.

"Mr. Blake." The voice comes again. Damn it, no.

Twenty-One

"Mikah." Again the voice comes. I slowly open my eyes. I'm back in the hospital room and a nurse wearing pale pink scrubs is standing over me.

"Huh?" I ask.

"Hi, Mr. Blake. Remember me?"

I look up into the soft round face of Vivienne's nurse from before. "Hi, Amanda."

"Hi there. I'm sorry to wake you, but we need to run some tests on Vivienne and shift her a little bit."

"Uh, sure." I stand up and push the chair back. "Can I stay?"

"Of course. Just step back, okay?"

I nod and step toward the foot of the bed. I notice that there is another nurse in the room with us. I rub my eyes to dispel the fog of sleep.

The moment I close my eyes, the dreaming sensation returns. I open them quickly, not wanting to slip back into that dream. Not just yet. I look at my right arm for the tattoo from the dream, but there is nothing there. I let out a long exhale.

Amanda and the other nurse go about their business. I watch as they check a couple of things on the monitors, but when they turn her onto her left side, my heart starts to race. Amanda holds her while the other nurse puts the stethoscope to Vivienne's back. She moves it around a couple of times and nods to Amanda, and they lay her back down.

The other nurse, whose name I can't see, continues to go about checking things as Amanda comes over to me.

"She's doing alright. Her vitals look good. You seem to have a profound effect on her heart when you're around." She smiles at me and I return a quizzical look. "Dr. Alston told me, and I can see the snap shot on the monitor." She smiles again. "Her lungs are clearing up, which is a good thing, and she doesn't seem to be in any pain right now." I nod. "Have you had dinner?"

I look at my watch. It's nearly six. "No, but Red should be bringing some food shortly. Thank you."

"Of course."

She turns to go back to the bed to finish up.

"Oh, I almost forgot," I say. "The number over on that monitor. Is that the baby's heart rate?"

She looks over to the monitor and back at me. "It sure is."

"Is that...normal?"

She smiles. "That is a great number to have up there. Babies' hearts beat far faster than ours do. The monitor will go off here and at the nurse's station if the rate drops below one thirty five. Which is still in the normal range, but we want to keep a very close eye on it."

I nod. I'm not normally this speechless when it comes to things, but all this medical stuff is so foreign to me.

"If the heart rate drops, it may also be a sign that Vivienne is in distress."

"Okay. This is all so out of my area of expertise." I feel helpless right now, and asking these questions is the only thing I can think of that might help me feel more in control of a situation I clearly have no control over.

"That's why we're here, Mr. Blake," the nurse behind Amanda says.

"Thank you," I say. They both gather up their equipment and head for the door.

"Do you need anything, Mr. Blake?"

"Mikah. And no, I'm fine. Thank you."

"Of course, Mikah. If that changes, go ahead and press the button on the remote on the bed and we'll do what we can."

"Thanks again."

She nods and ducks out the door.

I look back at Vivienne. This is going to be a very long road, and I am not a very patient person. It nearly killed me to give Vivienne the space she wanted after the last time we were here, and the only reason I did it was because I knew that I'd pushed her beyond her limits. After leaving her room that day, I researched post-traumatic stress disorder and, while I'm no expert, I see now what I did wrong. Given the chance again, I won't make the same mistake twice.

Although I'm still tired, and on top of that have a burning need to see what will happen next in the vision, I decide that it's best not to shut my eyes yet. I'm pretty sure Red will be here before long, and I'd much rather have some uninterrupted time to see where this is going.

I make a quick trip to the bathroom and then grab my laptop and head back to the chair, placing my computer between me and the armrest, facing Vivienne. She looks the same: peaceful.

When I gently touch the back of her hand, I'm momentarily taken aback by how warm her skin feels, but that is more than likely a good thing. Once the shock wears off, I notice that there is an unfamiliar pulse that runs through my body. But this time it's not from my back; it's from my heart.

A couple of weeks ago, this beautiful woman waltzed into my life. A life I'm not sure I'm familiar with anymore. Nothing is as it seemed. I'm not sure how I feel about all this angel nonsense, but I have the distinct feeling that I don't have a say in the matter.

The unwelcome realization hits me: If I want to be with Vivienne, I'll have to tell her about this angel business. What if she thinks I'm crazy? What if she doesn't want anything to do with me?

I sink back into the chair, staring hard at her beautiful, bright red, curly hair. Her face. What I wouldn't give to see those beautiful, ice-blue eyes, warm and full of wonder.

What am I bringing her into? What if what I'm facing is too dangerous for her? What if I'm leading her down a path that she isn't meant to go?

I can't stay away from her – that much is obvious – and more than that, I've been charged with protecting her. How on earth am I supposed to do that?

Twenty-Two

A sudden knock on the door causes me to jump clean out of my chair. I'm on my feet, fists clenched at my side, but the absence of the buzz in my back does not go unnoticed as the door clicks open.

"Mikah," says a male voice – one that is familiar, but in my moment of panic, I can't place it.

"Yeah!" I say, clipped.

"It's Detective Stevens. Can I come in? I'm off duty. I came by to check on you and to see Vivienne." His voice is calm, casual, almost friendly.

"Come in."

I look down at Vivienne and become conscious once again of the sucking and pulling of the ventilator. She hasn't changed; she's still sitting there, empty.

"My God." I hear him exhale, and I look to my left. Detective Stevens is wearing blue jeans and a navy blue MPD t-shirt, tucked in. I notice he is without his gun. I turn back to Vivienne and take my seat again.

"Have you captured Riley?" I ask. I'm pretty sure I know the answer to that question, but I have to ask it anyway.

"Not that I should be telling you this, but no. We have not."

I bristle at this. "I can be a very valuable asset in your search for him. It's to both our benefit for you to share information with me."

"I'm not here to argue or pick a fight, Blake. I came to see Vivienne. Whether you believe it or not, I care about her," he says. I can hear the sadness in his voice.

"You care, but yet you let this happen?" I ask, still looking at Vivienne. It's unfair and I know it, but seeing her like this....

"Blake, we both know how this happened, and I can't turn back time, I can't bring my officer back any more than I can make Vivienne's injuries go away." The more he talks, the more sadness filters into his voice.

"I know," I say. I lean forward, putting my elbows on my knees and my head in my hands.

Neither one of us says anything else for a few minutes. Finally I stand and gesture for him to sit: my peace offering. I go to the opposite side of the bed and sit by her feet, careful not to jostle her. I gently rub along her leg and fight the urge to smile as the heart monitor goes nuts.

"She's like a daughter to me," Stevens says. "After seeing her in the hospital the last time, I did my best to keep tabs on her. I spoke with Al."

"Who's Al?"

"The gentleman who drives the bus that she normally takes home after work. I told him to keep a good eye on her because I wasn't always able to do so."

"How did Rebecca Black get to her?"

I'm genuinely curious, not accusing, but his head shoots up and he looks hard into my eyes. "We weren't looking for her. Didn't know we needed to be looking for her. It wasn't until one of our drug task force guys noticed Riley coming and going from a well-known drug neighborhood that we started to get suspicious that he was up to no good. At the time that Rebecca was in Vivienne's diner, Riley was in North Minneapolis. We had no reason to suspect that he would send someone else to talk to her." He takes a deep breath and rubs his face.

"The task force was working on trying to catch him on drug-related charges. They had intel on Riley that pointed to him wheeling and dealing. They tried a couple of times to pull him over or pick him up, but each time they had nothing to go on, and the worst we could charge him with was speeding." He rubs at the stubble on his chin. "We lost track of him the night of Rebecca's murder and haven't been able to pinpoint him since."

Twenty-Three

The Detective finally leaves when Red arrives with food. Red hands me a large, surprisingly heavy picnic basket. "Celeste insisted that you would prefer this to something from a restaurant, which is why I'm so late, but I can go get you something else. I don't mind at all."

Puzzled, I open the basket to find French bread, a large bag of potato chips, two containers of fresh fruit, and a container of her amazing chicken salad. I smile.

"I guess maybe I was wrong," Red adds when he sees my smile.

"This," I say, pointing to the basket, "is beyond comparison. No restaurant food could come close."

Further exploration of the basket uncovers a thermos of coffee - no doubt the way I like it - and two cans of Mountain Dew. I shake my head at the latter: my one not-so-healthy vice in this world. There are also napkins, plates, and utensils.

"She's thorough," I mutter as I close up the basket.

"That she is. You really should eat something," Red says, eying the basket as I put it on the floor.

I nod absently and take my seat back on the bed at Vivienne's feet. "I will."

"Yes, sir. I don't mean to meddle."

I roll my eyes and shake my head at him. As annoying as it can be sometimes, his so-called meddling is what gets me places, allows me to do things, and makes sure that everything runs smoothly. "I enjoy your meddling, Red. It's alright."

"Has there been any change?" he asks, looking at Vivienne.

Shaking my head, I say, "No, but Amanda - one of her nurses - was here again about twenty minutes ago. Said that Dr. Alston will be up shortly. I'll try and eat after she leaves."

"Fair enough." Red smiles, but I can tell he is watching me carefully. Looking for something, or making sure I'm really as okay as I say I am. "Do you need anything else?"

I quickly run through a list of possibilities. "Besides her better, I'm not sure."

"Understandable, though I cannot help with that. As much as I would like to."

"I know. I'm alright for now."

"Very well. I'm only a phone call away. I'll come back in the morning."

I look at my watch and realize that it is after eight. "Alright, we'll see you in the morning then." I nod at him.

He nods back, takes a look a Vivienne, then turns and silently slips from the room.

I stay sitting on the bed with my hand gently rubbing along her leg and watch the monitor. The longer I keep my hand on her leg, the less crazy the monitor gets. Which is probably a good thing because I don't need anyone telling me that I can't touch her. The thought sends a shiver through my body, and suddenly my back has come alive once again.

This time, it's different. My emotions are heightened by a desire that I haven't felt in a long time. I try in vain to shake it off, but I can't. My heart aches with a need to be near her, to hold her, to touch her, to—

Oh, no, you don't.

I stand and make a beeline for the bathroom, quickly shutting the door behind me. I grip the sides of the sink hard, hoping that the pain in my hands will drive away the unexpected, unwelcome erection.

"Damn it," I curse under my breath, gritting my teeth and squeezing my eyes shut. But my back vibrates with excitement as I grow harder and the need grows stronger. If this desire doesn't die down soon on its own, I'm going to have to make it go away.

When I finally open my eyes and look into the mirror in front of me, they are electric blue, intense with arousal.

I feel the back of my shirt push outwards, away from my body. I reach for the hem and pull it up over my head.

Placing my hands back on the counter, I lean forward, eyes closed, trying to think about anything nonsexual. But everything I think of turns sexual in some form or another. Planes, cars and trains? Excellent places to have.... I drop that thought quickly, as it's only egging me on. The stock market? Up and.... Nope. Work? Nope. Vivienne? Hell, no.

Little by little, I can feel my body calming. Without Seraphina around, I don't know how else to do this. I quickly shift the image in my head to that of Rebecca Black and the video I watched this morning, but before it gets too involved, that sense of fullness associated with Seraphina comes over me and I hear her voice, singing the same gentle melody as before.

Thank stars. It took you long enough.

"Now, now, young angel. I was giving you a chance to rectify the situation yourself, which you had obviously started to do so well. Not the images I would have chosen to use to calm myself, but it worked nonetheless. Now to settle those wings of yours."

My head flies up and my eyes open. After I removed my shirt, I became more interested in calming my erection than the possibility that my wings were coming out. I lean forward slightly so that I can see over my shoulders, and I can instantly see what she's talking about. Coming from my back are the white tips of feathered wings. My eyes widen in shock as I watch them slowly retreat. Once my back becomes flat again, I feel a light clicking within my body. A lockdown on my back.

Thank you again.

"In due time you will learn to manage this yourself. I'm rather impressed that you were able to stop the full spread from happening. Though I would imagine the time is coming where we need to work on letting them out and locking them down, provided you want to stay where you are."

"What is that supposed to mean?"

"You will need to learn to control your emotions, not allow your inner angel to get the best of you. If you don't, you will expose yourself to the world and to the demonic ones who surround you. One thing to remember is that instances of heightened emotion – whether it is happiness, sadness, or carnal desire – will cause your body to react differently." I watch in the mirror as my eyes flash to black and back to their normal greenish-blue again.

"Relax, young angel. They cannot harm you unless you expose yourself to them."

Knowing that certain highly emotional situations could bring about this kind of reaction will help me better understand what can trigger an unexpected response. Knowing this will help me be more conscious of my reactions.

The thrum in my back flares and settles just as fast.

"Your doctor friend is coming," Seraphina adds, and she quickly retreats.

I take a big, long breath and reach for my shirt.

Twenty-Four

I step out of the bathroom to find Dr. Alston and Amanda looking over Vivienne.

"Hi," I say and try to smile as Dr. Alston looks up.

"Hey, Mikah. We're just checking her vitals and making some notes. Amanda tells me that Vivienne is responding to your touch?"

I blush. "My voice too, I think."

Amanda lets out a snort. My head turns in her direction and then follows her line of sight to the monitor.

"I'll say." Amanda retorts. "That is by far the strangest thing I've ever seen. What makes it even stranger is that you hardly know this girl and vice versa, and she has this completely subconscious reaction to your presence. But it also means that things are not as damaged up there as we first thought."

"What does that mean?" I ask.

"It means that we could probably bring her out of the coma right now and yield a pretty positive result." Dr. Alston says very matter of fact.

"So why don't you?"

She smiles back at me. "Well, two reasons. One, the coma is keeping her in one place and allowing her shoulder, lung, ribs and wrist to heal better. And two, I think we should wait at least another twelve hours, run a CT and make sure that we're not jumping the gun on the swelling."

"Alright," I say. I heard what she said, but I'm not sure it is registering properly. I want Vivienne to wake up sooner rather than later, but it really needs to be on her terms. But I also feel a little relieved that, with any luck, she will be awake sometime tomorrow. "What else can I do for her?"

"Well, nothing really. Sit here and talk to her. Or go home and get some rest." Seeing me scowl at that second option, Dr. Alston adds, "Or eat something, take a walk, or find something to read or talk to her about. Regardless, if she is having that kind of subconscious reaction to your presence, I wouldn't recommend leaving. It's obvious that it is helping her."

"I feel so helpless though."

"That makes two of us. All we can do right now is wait. It sucks, I know, but all her vitals are good, and the baby is doing great, all things considered. Some more time to heal is all she needs right now, and that is something we can all give her."

I nod in agreement, though I'm not sure this conversation has made me feel any better.

After a couple more minutes, they finish up. Dr. Alston and Amanda are leaving the hospital for the night, but the nighttime nurses have specific instructions to call immediately if anything changes. I'd honestly be surprised if Dr. Alston is really leaving the hospital instead of taking up residence in her office.

Once I make up my cot, I look dubiously at the basket Red brought in and decide that I can't really eat anything right now. The idea of having a meal, here in Vivienne's room without her, is unsettling.

I sit back down in the chair next to her bed. Resting my head next to hers, I start to play with a strand of her hair. I start thinking about the last time we were here. And how we got here.

I don't know what came over me that day, but something kept nagging at me to get her to a hospital, have her checked out, make sure she was okay. I try not to smile at the memory. She is like a kitten that thinks she's a tiger, and it is one of the many things that attracted me to her.

I never expected her to kick me out that day. Again, my need to protect her overcame any other rational emotion, and I pushed too hard.

The minutes that followed killed me. I paced around the emergency room, hoping that maybe she would ask me to come back. Then I saw Alston and a couple other nurses running toward her room. When I got back to the door, a nurse stopped me from going in. I paced. I hadn't a clue what was going on.

Eventually Dr. Alston emerged and explained what happened and what they were going to do at that point. I felt better knowing she was doing better, but guilt quickly set in because I realized that I was the cause of that. I don't know what set her off – whether it was a trigger or me leaving.

"I'm here. I'm not going anywhere," I say as I lift my head and gently kiss her forehead. "I miss your baby-blue eyes. Come back to me. Please."

Twenty-Five

I stay by her side for another minute or so, kiss her forehead once more, then grab my phone from the bedside table and go sit on the cot.

Turning my phone back on – I'd turned it off when I came into Viv's room – I silence the ringer and check my email. There are several emails from Jack, ranging in subject from video footage to other, non-Riley related information. There's one from my assistant, letting me know she's cleared my calendar for the next three weeks, and an email from Sydney – who is not only one of my business partners but also a very good friend – letting me know she's got things covered in my absence.

A second email from Sydney captures my attention. The subject line reads *Elton Bennett.*

Mikah,

Elton is on a warpath – he's attempting to destroy MSBE. We're choosing, at this time, to maintain a low profile and let him run his mouth in hopes that he digs his own grave. I have John and Phil working on maintaining our relationships with our top clients. The remaining managers are working on the rest. The general consensus among our top companies is that Elton is an idiot.

However, we've prepared our own team to defend at a moment's notice, and legal's working on a defamation suit against him.

Will keep you updated as more develops.

Regards,
Sydney A. Harper
Sr. Vice President
M.S. Blake Enterprises
Minneapolis, MN

I shake my head. Elton is a ruthless businessman who will stop at nothing to get what he wants. Right now, what he wants is to save his own ass. Without MSBE, the bulk of the funding for three very large, very expensive condo projects in Minneapolis is gone.

His phone call earlier today proves that he's pissed and will do whatever it takes. But does that include murder? Is it really possible that he is behind his son in all this mess?

I shake my head. I don't want to think about all that right now.

I put down the phone and look over toward Vivienne lying in the bed, seeming peaceful. I wish I knew whether or not she is resting comfortably.

I've been tuning out her ventilator, but now it catches my attention once again. I look over towards it. It's an innocent machine, but I have an image of something that looks a little like a cloth accordion lengthening and contracting as it presses air in and pulls it out. The sound is mesmerizing, and before I know it I'm lulled into a trance-like state, dreaming once again.

Twenty-Six

The air is shifting around me, light and gentle across my overly sensitive skin. I open my eyes to find myself back in the white room, looking through a tall, narrow window at a man with tanned skin, black hair and electric blue eyes.

On his back are a massive pair of pure-white, feathered wings in full extension. The wingspan alone has to be eight feet, if not more. The right-hand side of his chest and his right shoulder and arm are covered in an intricate black tribal tattoo, similar to the one I saw previously.

I stumble backwards as I realize it's not a window. It's a full-length mirror, and the winged, tattooed man is me. I watch my reflection try to regain its balance. The weight of the wings on my back finally registers, and I'm briefly knocked around as I try to stabilize.

"Easy there, angel. You're alright." This beautiful voice coming from behind me can only belong to one person. I feel my knees buckle again. This time, I'm a little more prepared for it and I don't lose my balance.

"What's happening to me?" I ask, but she doesn't answer.

I flex my shoulders and the wings shift. I try, for curiosity's sake, to pinpoint the muscles in my back where the wings are. I find them, push them downward, and instantly the wings follow suit. They've gone down enough that I can see Vivienne standing behind me. Instinctively I shrug, and the wings come back up, taking her out of my line of sight. She giggles behind me and I smile. Repeating the same motions as before, I lower them again and pull inward, and the wings fold in. Vivienne is looking at me appraisingly for the work I've managed to accomplish. I smile at her.

Her face lights up and I start to turn toward her, but she stops me by saying, "No, no. Keep facing the mirror. Keep practicing."

My heart sinks. I want to hold her, to touch her, but instead I do as she's asked and turn back toward the mirror. I push the wings back out, marveling at the fluid motion and at the force of air that comes from them.

"Can I fly?" I ask her.

"Yes, in time." Her voice is soft, approving, and much closer than before.

Then it happens – so fast that I'm not entirely sure what's happened – but my wings shiver, sending a rapid pulse of pleasure through my body. "Ahh!" I moan. And the sensation comes again. My wings go limp, and through hooded eyes, I see Vivienne standing behind me. She is smiling, happy.

She strokes my wing again. I don't know how much I can hold back and I moan again. She moves away - I feel the air shift in her wake - and I'm lost and empty without her touch. I close my eyes.

A warm, soft finger trails along my jaw. I lift my chin. Her touch has left a searing desire in its path.

"Keep them closed," she says softly.

"But I need to see you," I say, hoping the need in my voice conveys the feelings running through me. Each emotion, every sensation, is heightened beyond anything I've ever felt before.

I feel a whoosh of air go past me. My wings? But they're in the same position, still unmoving.

"Open your eyes, Mikah." Her voice is sweet and warm. I attempt to obey, but I can't seem to bring my eyes to open.

"Mikah." I feel a nudge at my shoulder. "Come on, Mikah, wake up."

Still I can't open my eyes. "Mikah." A deeper tone.

Twenty-Seven

My eyes fly open to see Red standing over me, and I jump and slide away from him. Sweat rolls off my forehead.

"It's alright, lad, it's just me."

I plop back down onto my pillow. "You really need to stop waking me up," I grumble.

He laughs. "Interrupting a good dream?"

"Yes." I groan.

I want to shout at him, but it seems that this dream is going to continue until it draws to its conclusion, so eventually, when I close my eyes again, with any luck it will come back.

"Sorry. Dr. Alston will be here in a couple of minutes. You've been sleeping like the dead, it's nearly ten in the morning." Holy shit. I can't believe I've been asleep for nearly twelve hours. "They've already taken Vivienne for a CT and some additional tests and brought her back again. The doctor will be here soon to talk to you."

"Shit." I climb out of bed quickly, looking in Vivienne's direction as I stumble to the bathroom.

When I come out a few minutes later after having freshened up as best I could with cold water from the sink, Red has made up the cot, so I take a seat on the end of Vivienne's bed.

Red hands me a travel mug and I take a sip.

"Thanks for the coffee."

"Any change?" Red asks, gesturing toward Vivienne.

"Not that I'm aware of. They didn't wake me, so I'm assuming no." I take another sip of coffee. "What time did you get here?"

"Around seven. I figured you wouldn't have slept much last night and that you would be awake. It was a few minutes after that they came for Vivienne and took her for tests. I stayed because I figured if you woke up you'd likely panic, and I didn't want you freaking out the staff. They only brought her back about thirty minutes ago."

I let out a soundless chuckle and bob my head. "You do know me well, don't you."

My back buzzes quickly and calms just as fast, just like it did yesterday when Dr. Alston was coming. Let's see if it is the same as before.

After a few heartbeats the door clicks open, followed by the clacking of heels on the linoleum floor.

"Good morning, Mikah. Red." She is wearing a black dress, black nylons and black heels.

I cock an eyebrow at her.

"I had a private appointment this morning and haven't changed." She laughs a bit.

I smirk at her and she smiles a little wider.

"So what's the verdict, Doc?"

"Well, the swelling in her brain has completely diminished, which is beyond what we thought would happen. Also, her lung and her shoulder look great. I'm a little perplexed about her wrist, though."

I raise my eyebrows at her. "How so?"

99

"Well, there seems to be very little sign of swelling underneath the brace she's in. It's not normal." She shrugs like it's no big deal.

"Maybe she's a fast healer."

She snorts. "Maybe, but this is beyond fast healing." She just shrugs again, and I make a mental note to ask Seraphina about Dr. Alston.

"Ask me what?" It's not Dr. Alston speaking now.

Where'd you come from?

"I've been here the whole time. I came in sometime around the time Red showed up."

How'd you not hear my question then?

She sighs. "Because I wasn't paying attention."

Alright then, give me a minute.

"So what now, Doctor?"

"Well, we are going to pull back on her sedation and bring her out of the coma slowly. We will keep her on the ventilator until all the sedation medicine has stopped, which will take a couple of hours."

"Why so long?"

"We want to make sure that she doesn't come out of it too fast, it can cause undue harm or stress to her and her body. Doing it slowly allows her a better chance to come out of it on her own. When she's ready."

I nod slowly at her, trying to process all of this. "So now what do we do?"

"I'm going to go push a few buttons, and we wait," she says with some hope in her voice.

"What are the risks of bringing her out now instead of waiting a little longer?" I'm not sure I want to know the answer to this, but I have to ask.

"Minimal. But there is still a chance she might not come out of the coma for a couple of days, and...there is still a very small chance that she may never come out of it at all."

Twenty-Eight

My heart starts racing and my palms start sweating.

"Relax, Mikah." Dr. Alston and Seraphina say in unison. It's rather obnoxious and I have the sudden urge to yell jinx.

Seraphina laughs.

"I'm trying." I take a few deep breaths as Dr. Alston goes to work pushing buttons.

"I'm going to have Amanda come in with some new fluids and take some vitals in about twenty minutes, then about every thirty minutes or so after that. We will also be monitoring for signs of discomfort. If she is in pain we may see her heart rate spike, and as she becomes more conscious, we'll see little things like finger twitches or a furrowing of her brow. If you see this, press the call button and we'll come in. Okay?"

"Okay," I say breathily.

"I have complete faith that she'll be alright. If I didn't, I would not be doing this now."

"Alright."

She grabs my shoulder as she passes and squeezes.

"You alright, sir?" Red chimes in. Jeez, I forgot he was here.

I turn to look at him. "Yeah, I think so. Listen. The other apartment downstairs, the one Celeste isn't using?"

"Yeah, the one across from me?"

"Right. Look, get in touch with Rusty and get them in that apartment. Make sure that everything is working properly, get the water turned on...you know the drill. She'll need a place to stay when she leaves the hospital and I'm no longer giving her a choice. Once we have a better idea of when she'll be released, we'll get it stocked up. Oh, and one last thing. Send Celeste on a shopping spree. Vivienne is going to need some new clothes, towels, linens, etcetera."

He nods. "Alright, we can handle that."

"Perfect. Thank you, Red. For everything."

"My pleasure, lad, you know that."

I nod and he leaves the room.

Are you still there?

I feel the fullness return once again. How does she do that?

"I'm here. I do that by becoming one with your angel self. Something you too will learn how to do eventually. I was here the whole time, just distantly communicating with you."

"See, and here I thought my head was my own when you weren't around."

She laughs. "Nope, I'm always connected. It's just a matter of whether or not I want to listen to you."

"Hardy-har. Alright. Dr. Alston. Is she familiar with all this angel, otherworldly stuff?"

"Not that I'm aware of. I can check. There are only a few common people that know – or at least think they know – that we exist. So it's unlikely that she does, but I will ask."

"No, it's alright. She was just a little too cool about fast healing. Did you have anything to do with Vivienne's healing?"

"Nuh-uh. Nope. That's all you."

"How me?"

"Your presence is enough. Your kindness, warm nature, your nurturing...and the fact that you're an angel of course helps, too."

"Huh?" I guess it is something else to add to my list of learning.

"Not really. I'm not entirely sure there is anything to learn. Her healing is a combination of just you being here supporting her and the natural aura of healing you possess as an angel." She sounds almost chipper. It's rather odd, given the circumstances.

Not wanting to discuss this any further because I'm not sure how much more of this I can handle right now, I slide off of the bed and head toward my bag.

I'm going to shower. Any chance you can scram?

She laughs and vacates. Her absence sends a chill through me. I look back to Vivienne, who is still unconscious.

Please let her wake up okay, I pray, and then add, *But not before I get back into her room.*

Twenty-Nine

After my shower, I start to pace, impatiently waiting for Vivienne to wake up. Around noon, Red brings me lunch from a restaurant near the house that I enjoy, but my nervous energy makes it hard for me to want to eat anything.

Finally I decide to distract myself with work. Not long after I've picked up my laptop and replied to a couple of emails, Sydney jumps on my case about working. I let out a nervous chuckle at her response and move onto the emails Jack has been sending me over the last twenty-four hours.

Information about Riley's background, Elton's background, some Riley sightings and a new batch of evidence on where he's possibly hiding. Jack is a real genius at tracking people. I have no doubt that at least half of the information he obtains is illegal, which is why we have to be careful about what we send on to Detective Stevens.

One of the emails catches my attention.

It's encrypted - for my eyes only. Unfortunately, I'm not equipped at the moment to open it, as I'm not sure of the level of security I have on the hospital's network. If he is sending this to me, it means he's found something important in relation to Riley or Elton. Which is good, but it could be pretty bad too.

After the voicemail from Elton yesterday, combined with Sydney's email, I begin to wonder, idly, what Elton is up to and how he plans to go about 'destroying me', as he so eloquently put it. Huh? I wonder if that's what Jack's email is about?

I try to push it from my mind entirely, and in doing so, it registers once again that all the humming is gone. Okay, maybe it's not gone, because I can still feel it slightly as I flex my back and shoulders. For now I'm going to take this as a positive sign that there is little to be concerned about right now.

Just as I think this, a prickling spreads across my skin. It's not painful, but rather it's pleasurable. Instinctively my eyes drift to Vivienne lying on the bed, and in the instant that I look at her, I see the corner of her mouth twitch slightly.

My heart swells to see some life in her face. Though her eyes are still closed, that twitch is more than I've seen from her in the last day, and I become hopeful that she is going to be alright.

I quickly close the laptop, set it aside and lean forward toward the bed.

"Vivienne." I gently place one hand on her upper arm and my other hand on her gorgeous red hair, stroking lightly. "Vivienne. Vivienne, can you open your eyes?" I pause a moment, waiting for a reaction.

There isn't one.

"Vivienne," I whisper.

Still no response.

I stay where I am, playing with her hair, until Dr. Alston comes in to check on her again.

Before I can tell her about the mouth twitch, Dr. Alston pulls up the blankets at the foot of the bed.

"What are you doing?" I ask a little defensively.

She doesn't flinch at my tone. "I'm looking for reflexes. To see if she has any reaction."

She takes a pen from her jacket and runs the top of the pen from heel to toe on one of Vivienne's feet.

We both watch intently.

After a heartbeat, Vivienne's toes curl in slightly.

I can't help the smile that spreads across my face.

Dr. Alston checks the other foot, and the end result is the same.

"What does this mean?"

She tries the first foot again and then the other before answering. "Right now it means that her brain is registering sensations."

"Is the delay in the reaction normal?"

"For now, yes. It really doesn't mean anything, only that she is still under the medication. Which is okay. As it wears off, that reaction should get a little faster."

I nod.

"Have you seen any movement?" she asks.

"A little while ago, I thought I saw her mouth twitch."

"It's not impossible. About another hour and the sedative should stop working altogether. Once we reach that point, I will be sending Amanda in here to keep a close watch on her vitals."

She moves around the bed, pulls the tape out from the fetal monitor and begins to look over it.

The action sends a shiver of excitement through me, and I'm not really sure why.

"What kind of plans have you made for her once she is released?" Dr. Alston peers at me out of the corner of her eye. "You know she can't go back to that apartment," she states matter-of-factly.

"I'm aware, but her will and determination are going to make it quite the battle."

She smiles at me. "But you're just the right person to argue with her."

I let out a breathy laugh. "You're right, I am. I have an additional condo in my building that's not being used. If I can't convince her to stay with me, she can live there until either she is back on her feet again or this whole mess is taken care of." As I say this, a sharp warning zing lights up my back, and I get the sudden impression that getting to the bottom of this mess is not going to be an easy task.

"Well, once she is fully recovered, I don't see any reason that she can't find a way to take care of herself. Whatever you do, don't stifle her. You might be able to get her to stay with you or to take that apartment, but whatever you do, make sure that she has the freedom to do things on her own. I could be wrong, of course, but she is very independent, and I don't see her changing that. So if you can help her while letting her make her own choices, she will be much better off." She puts down the tape and looks at me. "She needs help, counseling - especially that. I can take care of her physical medical needs, but you need to make sure that she sees a psychiatrist."

I nod, contemplating. "I wish I could just take it all away from her. All the memories, all the hardship she's endured. She deserves so much better than that."

"You're absolutely right, but we cannot change the things that have happened to her, we can only help her move forward."

She unwraps the stethoscope from her neck and holds it to Vivienne's chest.

I wonder idly if, when she's ready, I can convince Vivienne to work for MSBE.

I watch Dr. Alston move the stethoscope around, listening. When she is done, she pulls up the blanket to look at the incision on Vivienne's ribs. She pulls back the gauze.

"What the hell?" she says.

Thirty

"What's the matter?" A pulsing radiates throughout my entire body. It's the same sensation that came yesterday when I got really excited. Oh, no.

"Her incision."

I panic slightly. Fighting the sensations across my back, I stand up. "What's wrong with it?"

"Nothing."

I scowl at her.

"I mean, well, nothing is wrong except for the fact that it's..." She pauses and I lean over to look. "Come around, you can see better."

I sidestep the chair and the bed, walking around to come up on Dr. Alston's right.

"Look." She holds out her hand. A couple of thick staples rest on her palm.

I look at the area under the bandage. "What on earth? It's practically gone." In place of what was probably an angry red incision just yesterday is a faint, nearly perfectly healed line about an inch and a half long.

"I've heard of - and even seen - some fast healers, but I'll be damned if I've ever seen anything this fast." She slowly pulls the rest of the gauze aside and rolls Vivienne forward just a bit.

SERAPHINA! SERAPHINA! DAMN IT, WHERE ARE YOU?

My skin is on fire as I take in what is across her back. Suddenly it all clicks into place.

"Has that always been there?" I ask Dr. Alston.

"Has what?"

SERAPHINA!

Damn it. No wonder. "Nothing. Thought I saw something."

No Goddamn wonder why my parents could never get anyone to do anything about my back when I was a kid.

SERAPHINA!

They couldn't see it. I could see it. And Mom could see it, for reasons I now know. But Dad...did Dad ever see it? That would explain why he never asked to see my back after Mom died.

SERAPHINA! Now is not the time to disappear on me. I'm gonna wring her damn neck. *SERAPHINA!* Damn it, where is she?

"I'm going to order an x-ray of her arm and shoulder. See what is going on in there." I just nod and move out her way. "Hey, you okay?"

The excited pulsing has not calmed down one bit since I stood up a moment ago. "Yeah, why?"

"You look very distracted."

"I'm a little jolted by the whole healing thing."

"So am I. But I doubt that there is a test in the world that can tell me how or why. All I know is that it has and..." She just shrugs.

"You completely baffle me with your nonchalance. Most doctors would be thinking of a way to exploit a miracle like that."

She laughs. "Mikah, let me tell you something about that."

I sit gingerly on the side of the bed, giving her my full attention.

"I didn't go to medical school to be a doctor so that I could become rich and famous. I became a doctor because it gives me a great opportunity help those in need. I specialized in obstetrics because I love babies and I'm thoroughly fascinated by the way we grow and develop in the womb, but I don't think that the little miracles we see everyday are cause for exploitation. I will just be amazed by it. And maybe do a little research about it," she admits, "because eventually the curiosity will take over. But in the end, I will do nothing to take advantage of it. I've seen a lot in my time that I can't explain, and I'd rather spend my time on something that I can explain or fix than something that is solving itself." She smiles at me, warm and genuine.

"I wish there were more doctors like you."

She chuckles a bit. "I love my job. And her. I fell in love with her when she was here a couple of months ago. She is an intelligent, gorgeous young lady who deserves to have her past wiped away and a future that is bright and full of prosperity, hope and love. Never forget that, Mikah."

She places her hand on my shoulder, squeezes briefly. "She's an angel. She deserves to be treated like one," she says as she leaves the room.

"Oh, you have no idea how right you are," I mumble.

Then, in my loudest silent mental shout: *SERAPHINA!*

Thirty-One

Instantly my back is ablaze and the feeling of fullness has returned.

What the hell took you so long?

"What?"

I've been screaming for you for at least the last five minutes. What took you so long?

I can't shake the image of Vivienne's back from my mind.

Seraphina catches on to what I'm thinking about. "Vivienne?" she asks.

I turn back to the bed and pull back the covers, gently pushing her hip to move her forward.

Peeking out between the gaps of the hospital gown are clear markings of wings that resemble my own.

"Explain this to me?" I say aloud. "What on earth is going on with her?" *How is this even possible?*

"Sit down, young one, and I will show you."

I'd rather stand up.

"No, sit down and I will show you."

Reluctantly, I step back from the bed, walk back around to my chair and take a seat.

"Get comfortable. Relax."

Instinct has me on edge because I don't know what to expect. But I lean forward to rest my head on the bed. My right hand plays with a strand of Vivienne's hair while the other one is rests along her arm.

"Close your eyes."

I do as she tells me, but I can feel the anxiety rising.

"Relax, young angel. I will not harm you. You've already seen most of this."

The dreams? I relax almost instantly; this is something I've wanted to see since Red woke me up this morning. I take a deep breath, filling my lungs, and then slowly exhale.

Suddenly I'm back in the white room on my knees – I can feel the hard floor digging into them. I open my eyes.

Standing behind me is a beautiful, pale-faced Vivienne, her red hair curling down her back, bright against all this white. Atop her head is a tiara, resting right along her hairline. In the center of the circlet is a shiny white opal surrounded by a beautiful silver Celtic design that extends into her hair.

My heart melts. She is simply stunning.

Her dress is white, with silver accents along the bodice. The design is flowery, with a beaded band directly below her breasts. Two thin straps, accented with the same style of beadwork, go up and over her shoulders. Coming off the straps is sheer chiffon that extends down beyond my line of sight.

Looking a little closer, I see that she looks healthier, filled out in her face, and her arms look well toned.

"You look beautiful, *A chuid den tsaol.*" My voice is not what I expect to hear; it has an echoing quality.

She smiles back at me in the mirror. "Close your eyes."

I close my eyes and can feel her moving around me. Her hand trails feather-light along my wing; the pleasure it brings is breathtaking. She caresses my wing from where it comes out of my back all the way to the tip, and by the time she reaches the tip, I'm on the verge of losing control. But yet I feel rooted in my spot.

I feel the air shift as she comes to stand on my right. "Turn toward me."

With the sensation of her touch still pulsing through my body, it is hard to coordinate my movements and turn. I let my shoulders drop slightly, and I feel a rush of air as my wings fold inward. I lift my face but keep my eyes closed as I feel a finger trace lightly along the bridge of my nose down to the tip. Then her finger presses against my lip and I kiss the pad.

She gently lays her palm against my cheek. I lean into her touch, desperate to open my eyes, but I keep them closed, relishing the sensation of her warm touch against my skin. I raise my right hand and hold hers against my face, weaving my fingers in between hers.

"Keep your eyes closed and give me your hand," she says, the sound of bells in her voice.

I lift my hand slowly, remembering the way she's flinched before, but my caution proves unnecessary. I can feel her other hand shift, and then her knees rub along mine as she kneels.

She gently takes my other hand in hers and says, "Open your hand flat."

I do as she asks and she tugs on my arm. I feel her warmth beneath my fingers, and at my fingertips I can feel the cool metal of her circlet and her cheek pressing into my palm.

She leans into my touch.

My heart soars and warm tears stream down my cheeks as I take in the magnitude of the gesture: She's just allowed me to touch her face. I feel her fingers along the back of mine as she press my hand to her.

"Do not cry." I can hear the emotion in her voice, and a moment later I feel her own tears.

I release her hand against my cheek and bring it up to meet her other cheek. Eyes still shut, cupping her face in my hands, I rise up onto my knees.

I feel a soft nudge against my stomach and then feel her press into me. My body becomes a live wire as our bodies draw closer to each other.

She lifts her chin.

I slowly lower my mouth, seeking hers.

When we connect, a surge of pleasure and hope courses through my body; it is almost uncontrollable.

She presses her hands against mine for a moment, holding them against her cheeks, and her fingers weave in between my own. I can feel her tug slightly as I kiss her again, lingering longer this time. Then she pulls my arms past her shoulders until they bump into something behind her. She slowly lowers my hands onto an object. The surge of desire flies through me once again as I come in contact with something hard surrounded by soft velvet.

My eyes fly open and I gasp. "Vivienne."

"Don't stop," she says breathily, and I gently slide my hands along the pure white feathers of her wings.

Looking down at her, reality becomes clear. This is the future. Our future.

"She will be our *banphrionsa*." The voice that comes now is not Vivienne's but a different female voice that comes with some sense of recognition, but yet not familiar.

"Princess?" How is this even...

I let the thought trail away and close my eyes. When I open them again, Vivienne has vanished. I turn quickly, looking for her, and realize that my wings have also gone.

I spin back around. In the spot where Vivienne stood just a moment ago is another woman. A familiar woman.

I stumble backwards.

"Mom?"

"Yes, baby." Her voice radiates with emotion.

I can't speak as I steady myself, looking again at the beautiful woman standing before me. She looks amazing. Her gorgeous blonde hair, bright blue eyes, and soft features are warm and inviting. She looks years younger than the pictures I have, almost like a teenager.

"How?" I finally manage to breathe.

In answer, she spreads her wings. "I am like you, my son. I too am an angel. Which is how you have become one."

"But..." I have no words, and I crumple to the floor on my knees and sit back on my feet, my hands balling into fists against my thighs.

"There is much to learn, *A leanbh*, but your love is in danger, and you are the only one who can save her. The child she caries is the key to restoring the natural order bestowed upon us as *aingeal*. There is an imbalance among our kind, made worse by the *foinse olc*, the source of evil, as Satan too will breed with one that will stand by his side no matter what.

"Your need for her is strong, your hope for her burns bright and hot. She needs you to help her, to guide her. She is pure. Despite the life she's led, she is pure of heart. Never doubt that."

The breath moving in and out of my lungs is thick. "She gives me hope."

"As she should, my son. She should give you reason to be whole and pure yourself. You, too, know hardship. Your father did all he could for you and our family, but raising children was not his strength in life. You were forced to do it alone. Without me."

I snort a laugh. This is all too much to handle.

"There is much more to learn, but know that we are here, we will help you, and when you return home, I will see to it that you have our histories at your disposal. It will help you understand your purpose. And ours..."

Her voice trails off at the end and I look up.

She's gone once again.

Thirty-Two

I put my head in my hands. This is too much. All this angel stuff is too much to understand all at once. I don't know how I'm going to handle all of this without going crazy. It's surreal.

Cool fingers on my cheek bring a zing of pleasure. Once again I put my hand over hers, only this time it's not the soft, warm touch of before. Her fingers are almost cold, and there is something hard and rough pressing into my cheek.

I let out a rushed breath and pull back, my eyes flying open. Bright, ice-blue eyes and a mess of beautiful red hair.

I stand up, stumble and fall back into the chair.

Her lips turn upwards in a smile behind the ventilator hose.

"Is that funny to you?" I laugh and smile at her.

She nods. Then tries to pull on the hose.

"Don't." I reach for her hands to pull them back. She doesn't flinch at my quick movements, and my heart swells once again. I take her hands in one of mine and pull the chair up close to her bed.

A hum of hope and life and undeniable pleasure radiates through me. "I missed you." The words are out before I can stop them.

A faint trace of a blush kisses her cheeks.

I notice that the natural light in the room has faded significantly. It's later than I would have thought possible.

"Are you in pain?"

She shakes her head slightly.

"I'm going to push the button for Amanda to come, okay?"

Her eyes widen in recognition.

"Yes, Dr. Alston and Amanda have been taking care of you."

She nods again, and I reach for the call button. As soon as I touch the button, there's a commotion outside the room and the door clicks open.

Dr. Alston comes in first, followed by Amanda.

"Hello, Vivienne. Pleasure to see you again. Are you in any pain?"

I watch Vivienne shake her head. I can't take my eyes off of her. An overwhelming sense of joy is taking control of my body at the fact that she's awake.

She is looking at me, too.

Dr. Alston has gone to the fetal monitor again, looking over the last foot or so of tape. "How long has she been up?"

"I don't know, I was sleeping against her bed. She woke me up."

Vivienne pulls her hand from mine and holds up five fingers.

"Five minutes?" Dr. Alston asks. Vivienne nods, and Dr. Alston goes back to reviewing the tape.

I look up at the baby's monitor; the heart rate is around one-fifty. Curious, I look at Vivienne's monitor.

Sure enough, captured about five minutes ago, there is the now-familiar pattern of Vivienne's heartbeat when I'm around. I can't help but smile.

Vivienne's head moves in the same direction. I look at her and watch her roll her eyes. I laugh and she squeezes my hand. Her other hand goes back to the tube in her mouth.

"Not just yet," Dr. Alston says. "How do your ribs feel? Do they hurt?"

She wiggles in the bed just a little bit, then she shakes her head.

"What about your wrist, does it hurt?"

She flexes her fingers, rotates her wrist and shakes her head again.

"Is it really possible that she is healed already?"

"Yes." This time the voice is in my head. Seraphina again.

You know, you could make yourself known before answering my questions.

She laughs. "I was here when you went to sleep, remember? Not my fault if you forgot."

Fair enough.

"Viv, how does your neck feel? Does it hurt?"

She scowls at the question then she shakes her head. I'd forgotten all about the bruises around her neck. Had I remembered those, then I'd have seen, like I do now, that the marks are much fainter than they were yesterday.

"Is she still on pain meds?" I ask, and Vivienne's eyes meet mine again.

"She's on a light dose of pain meds. But I'd be able to tell if she was giving me the runaround so I'd take out the tubes. She didn't even flinch." She turns to Vivienne. "Alright, Vivienne, we will take out the tubes. On one condition?"

She nods at Dr. Alston but is still looking in my direction.

"You don't go running a marathon at least for a few days."

I laugh out loud and see Vivienne's eyes scrunch up and her shoulders shake with laughter, though she doesn't make a sound.

"Mikah, I need you to move so Amanda can get in over there."

I watch Vivienne scowl at Dr. Alston, and I laugh again at her expression.

Dr. Alston laughs in return. "He's not going anywhere. We just need the room, okay?"

She nods reluctantly.

I stand up and sidestep Amanda's approach, taking a seat at the end of the bed near Vivienne's calves.

Amanda has gone to work pulling back some of the tape holding the tubes in place.

"Alright, Vivienne. Go ahead and breathe through your nose."

Amanda reaches over and turns off the machine.

"Now I need you to take a big, deep breath through your nose and hold it, and then on the count of three, I want you to exhale as hard and fast as you can. Are you ready?"

Vivienne nods.

"Okay, breathe in."

With the machine off the room is silent, and I hear the air enter though her nose, past the pipe. She scowls a little at the fullness of her lungs.

"One, two, three."

Thirty-Three

On three I hear Vivienne's rushed exhale. At the same time, Amanda holds down Viv's shoulders and Dr. Alston pulls on the tube.

Then Vivienne starts coughing and wincing slightly. The coughing lasts for a few moments.

"Water?" Vivienne says in a raspy voice when she's recovered.

Amanda is quick to grab the cup she brought in a few moments ago.

"Ice chips," she says as I take the cup from her, and then she presses the button on the side of the bed to raise Vivienne to a sitting position.

"Hi, there," I say, handing Vivienne the ice chips.

"Hi," she says, still raspy.

"How you doing?"

She nods and puts a couple of pieces of ice into her mouth. "I'm okay."

"Vivienne, how are you feeling? Any pain?"

She shakes her head. "No, but I'm really hungry."

I smile.

So does Dr. Alston. "We can work on that."

"How long...?" She trails off, clears her throat.

"It's Saturday." Dr. Alston pauses to look at her watch. "Seven twenty in the evening. You've been out since you came in yesterday morning."

Both Dr. Alston and I are watching for any reaction from Vivienne, who lets out a long breath.

"Is everything..." Her free hand reaches for her stomach, and relief washes over her face.

I can feel the emotion wrap around me, engulfing me.

"Everything looks good. You both are doing good."

Vivienne nods slowly, and then her eyes glass up.

"Can you guys leave us for a little while?" I ask Dr. Alston.

"Of course. Hit the button if you need anything, and we will get some dinner up here."

"No need. I'll take care of it. She deserves something better than hospital food."

Dr. Alston laughs. "This is true. Okay, but keep it light, like soup or broth." I nod. "I'll be back in shortly."

When the door clicks shut behind the doctor and nurse, I turn back to Vivienne, and she mouths, "Thank you."

"Of course."

I don't say anything more. I'm not going to force her to talk. I get up to get my phone.

"Where are you going?" she asks.

I turn back to her and smile. "Getting you some dinner."

"Oh."

I smile a little wider and call Red.

"Hello, sir."

"Hi. She's awake and she's hungry. Can you bring us both something, but keep it light and soft, like soup?"

"Of course. Celeste's already got some stuff going, in anticipation of her waking up. I'll be there shortly."

"Thanks, Red. If you could, leave it with the staff and have them bring it in."

"Absolutely. Call if you need anything else."

"Actually, can you bring me one of my t-shirts and a pair of sweatpants?"

"For you, sir?"

"No, for Vivienne. I think she'd be more comfortable." I look to her and she nods.

"We have clothes for her here if you'd like."

I hadn't realized they'd gotten that far already. "Pants. But bring one of my t-shirts."

"On it. See you soon."

"Yup." I hit the end button.

I turn back to Vivienne. "Red will be here soon with some food."

"Thanks."

"Anything, anytime." I pause. "How are you doing?"

She just shakes her head.

"I won't pry, but if you need to talk about something, I'm here. I'll listen."

"It's not that, really. It's more that...I'm trying to figure out how I ended up here," she says softly.

"Are you sure you want to talk about that?"

"No, but I know it's something I will need to know eventually." As she speaks, her eyes begin to droop.

"You're tired?" I ask.

She nods. "I am, but I'm confused."

"Is my being here making you uncomfortable?" Please, no. I don't want to leave.

She shakes her head. "I'm glad you're here." I walk toward the chair, but before I can sit down, she says, "I really need to go to the bathroom."

"You have a catheter." I try to not look at her, but I see the blush of embarrassment that spreads across her cheeks regardless. "I can call for Amanda."

"Nurse Fang," she says, and I laugh. "Go ahead." She smiles a little bit.

I reach for the button and a beep sounds over our heads.

"Yes, Vivienne?" Dr. Alston's voice.

"I need to go to the bathroom," she says, looking up toward the ceiling.

"I'll send Amanda in."

"Thanks."

A few moments later, Amanda comes into the room.

"How we doing, Viv?" she asks.

"Okay. I need to go to the bathroom and I don't want to use the catheter."

"Is it because he's in here?" She hitches her thumb in my direction and I nearly blush, embarrassed myself.

"I can step out," I say to Vivienne.

"No, I just want to go to the bathroom. Can't I just go?"

"Alright, but you can't get mad at me if we have to put it back in. Fair enough?" Vivienne just shrugs. "Mikah, can you give us some privacy?"

"Uh, sure." I turn on my heel and head toward the door.

"Don't go far," I hear Vivienne say.

"Right outside the door."

Thirty-Four

I wander aimlessly into the empty waiting room a couple of doors down from Vivienne's room.

A warm tingling sensation spreads and then quickly subsides before giving way to the tingling I'm most familiar with: icy stabbing sensations. I try in vain to not arch my back and curl in on the feeling, but it's hard; it hurts like hell.

I hear the chime of the elevator followed by footsteps. I reach into my pocket and press a button on my phone.

Scuff. Thud. Scuff, click. The door closes.

Someone is walking across the floor behind me. The icy stabbing continues as I realize the person behind me is a threat. The hairs on the back of my neck stand on end.

I spin around, preparing to defend against whatever is coming after me.

"Well, well, well. Look at what we have here."

My heart pumps faster and bright red rage fills my vision as I take in the man before me. The icy stabbing flares momentarily then settles. My veins almost feel frozen, but the feeling brings about an unusual sense of strength and I flex involuntarily as I grit my teeth. "What the hell are you doing here, Elton?" I spat at him.

"I heard your girlfriend was in the hospital and that you were hiding out here."

"Why are you looking for me?" I ask him. I know from his voicemail that he knew about Vivienne, in some fashion. Though I'm not sure if he knew, at the time, that she was alive. Has he put two and two together? Does he know that his son is responsible for the state of my 'girlfriend' as he puts it?

"We have something in common." He straightens his stance and his tie, a gesture that strikes me as ridiculous here in this context.

"And that is what, exactly?"

"Your little girlfriend is causing quite a problem for my family."

Rage flares hotter, brighter. "How do you suppose that is?"

"Well she broke up with my son. They were supposed to be married soon."

"Ha!" I bark at him. "That is the biggest line of bullshit I've ever heard. Though I'm curious, is your coming here your idea, or is it Riley's?" He doesn't respond. But I'm going to see where this goes. Elton could be the key to finding out where Riley is. "Your son seems to think he can control you too. So let me put it to you this way. My 'girlfriend,' as you call her, almost died because of the damage your son inflicted on her."

His eyes widen marginally. "How dare you accuse my son of beating a woman! That's preposterous!" His face begins to turn red. "He was in the process of getting her back, bringing her back to him."

"Wow Elton, you really are dense on so many levels. Did you not just bail your son out of jail for domestic violence?"

"It was a misunderstanding."

"Jesus, you make me sick. First, you post bail for your son who was arrested following the brutal beating of the woman you say he was trying to get back. The woman he beat to near death again Thursday night that fought for her life, and the life of your unborn grandchild."

"That's preposterous! She was never in the hospital. It was a misunderstanding."

"Jesus H-Christ Elton, wake the fuck up. Here's a thought for you. Why don't you go grab your son and walk into the downtown office of the MPD. See how they react to your son's arrival on their territory. If you're so inclined to find out the truth, that just might be the quickest, most efficient way to know for sure."

His face turns redder by the second. A career businessman hoping for a career in politics doesn't want to have this kind of negative publicity looming over his head.

"Did you know that your son is wanted for questioning in the murder of a twenty-three year old girl named Rebecca Black?" Deeper red. "Not to mention the brutal beating of a twenty-two year old woman who went through hell and back to save her life."

Purple to blue, then back to red. He shakes his head. "I don't believe you," he spats at me.

"I don't care if you believe me or not, Elton. The point is, it always comes out in the end. So you can decide here and now what side you're going to take in this matter. If you choose Riley's, then I suggest you get the hell out of here and get to work. You have one hell of a conspiracy to try and cover up." I turn my back on him.

"She is a Goddamn liability," I hear him say.

Bright red rage twists me around and launches me back in his direction. He doesn't flinch or back away. As my fist connects with his jaw and nose, I hear the crunch of breaking bones. See the blood spray across the floor as he grabs his face.

"You son of bitch!" I rage. "How dare you speak of any human being that way! We do not live in a world where you eliminate people just because they don't fit into your business plan, Elton Bennett. I will see your son fry for what he's done, and I will gladly stand by to watch you take the fall with him."

Glaring at me, he spits blood and mucus onto the floor. "You're not old enough to understand the true meaning of business. Do not ever talk to me like that again. In business you do what needs to be done to survive." His face contorts and he bends over and dry heaves, no doubt from the pain. "You have a choice to make Blake. Either reinstate your investment or so help me God I'll have you arrested for assault and destroy MSBE."

"Bullshit! That does not include murder and my stance with your investments will never change." I peer through the window towards Vivienne's room and fight a grin from spreading across my face. The cops outside of her room are making show of looking at the ceiling and rocking on their heels. I stalk past him, push the crash bar on the door and step out into the hallway.

As the door clicks shut behind me, I reach into my pocket, remove my BlackBerry and press pause. At the touch of a couple more buttons, the recorded conversation is on its way to Detective Stevens's email.

Thirty-Five

As I approach Vivienne's door, Amanda comes back out of the room.

"She alright?"

"She's great. Stubborn as all hell, but she's doing good. She wants the sling to come off. Said her shoulder doesn't hurt. I told her that it was up to the doctor and that I would discuss it with her. I know that Alston wanted to take some x-rays, but when we went in to get her you were sound asleep on her bed, so we decided to wait. Once she's done that, she'll decide what to do next."

"Thanks, Amanda."

"Of course. Call if you need anything."

I go back into the room. The bed has been lowered again, and Vivienne's eyes are closed. What a difference watching her sleep now compared to before. Color has returned to her cheeks and the absence of the hoses makes her look human again.

Her cheeks are flushed. No doubt the trip to and from the bathroom was exhausting.

I quietly walk over to the chair and sit down.

"Don't pry with her."

Hello, Seraphina. I hadn't planned on it.

131

"I know, but she seems to be doing a pretty good job of suppressing what's happened. She does remember, but, no doubt due to the years of abuse she's faced, she's learned how to suppress much."

I'd already assumed that and it's the reason I'm not pressing. I know she will need to talk to the cops at some point, and I'd rather she save her energy for that conversation. I will make arrangements for her to meet with someone she can trust to discuss all this bottled-up trauma.

"Don't be surprised if she won't do it. She will when she is ready, and not before. But it will only come at a time and place she knows with absolute certainty she is safe. All I ask is that you give her some time to get there."

I roll my eyes. *I know, Seraphina, this is not my first rodeo. Are we forgetting my sister?*

I change the subject to avoid more lecturing I don't need. *So, that dream. What on earth was that all about?*

"Well, first of all, you weren't on earth." She laughs and I shake my head. "You were in Elysium."

Elysium Fields? As in Greek mythology, where you go when you die?

"The same, only we no longer call it *Fields*. The mythological definition of Elysium is ideal happiness, though that's not entirely accurate. It's a place where angels live. A place where you yourself can go anytime you wish. The souls of the dead do pass through Elysium, but they do not stay unless they have a predestined purpose for being there. Like your mother, for example. She passed into Elysium upon her death because it was where she was supposed to go."

What about my father?

"That is something you will need to discuss with your mother. It is not my story to tell. But your mother is free to pass between heaven – as you call it – and Elysium. You will likely be able to do the same, should you wish."

As I call it? What do you call heaven, if not heaven?

"It used to be known as *Aether*, though not many of us call it that anymore. If you know some of your Greek mythology, then you would know that *Aether* was the first of the elementals to be born and represents the purest life and happiness. In all honesty, heaven and *Aether* is really all the same. But where the angels gather is separate. Those in *Aether* do not pass into Elysium, and vice versa. Unless, of course, you are one of the Chosen, which I believe you are."

What makes you so certain about that?

"You will find out soon. It is not something I can tell you."

Bull— I stop myself.

She laughs. "No, really, I can't. I'm bound by restraints that prevent me from disclosing certain secrets, and that is one of them. Just like you are unable to tell anyone other than those of your own species that you're an angel. Try it sometime." She laughs again. "Okay, I'm going to go. Red will be here shortly, and I'm neglecting my chores."

She doesn't stick around long enough for me to argue. I feel the rush of her leaving my mind and body.

Thirty-Six

About thirty minutes later, Red arrives with dinner for Vivienne and me, and Amanda brings it in.

"How long has she been sleeping?"

"About half an hour. She was sleeping when I came back in after her trip to the bathroom."

"Oh, okay. I'd try and wake her so she can eat. Plus, Alston will be back in shortly. She was going to be on her way up after seeing a patient with a smashed in nose downstairs in the E.R.." She smirks at me in a I-know-what-you-did kind of way.

"Alright." I say quickly before I start laughing hysterically at the fact that Alston is more than likely treating Bennett's busted nose. I'm not sure what to make of his whole ordeal, but it proves my earlier theory about doing anything to get what he wants.

Amanda goes about checking the monitors and IV fluids.

Elton came here to try and 'convince' me to reinstate my investments, as if I would see things his way.

Amanda interrupts my thoughts. "She can start drinking water, too. The ice chips were a way for her to slow down her intake. Her throat is probably pretty sore and will be for a day or two."

I nod. "I'll keep an eye on her."

She smiles and leaves.

I gently stroke Vivienne's arm. "Vivienne," I say softly, and her eyes flutter. "Dinner is here."

Her eyes flutter again, but they don't open.

"Come on, sweetie." I rub her arm a little more and she finally, slowly begins blinking, waking up. "Hi, there."

She smiles. "Hi," she breathes.

"I have soup. Are you hungry?"

She nods and I go about unpacking the dinner Celeste sent over. She's included her creamy chicken noodle soup, minus the big noodles and hunks of chicken. Instead it is more of a broth. And she used little tiny ring noodles. There are also bread rolls and some crackers.

"Smells good," she whispers.

"Is your throat bothering you?"

She nods.

"The soup should help."

She nods again.

I pour soup from the thermos into one of the two bowls Celeste put in the basket. The soup is steamy and smells wonderful. I reach for the button to raise Vivienne up, and I notice as she tracks my hand's movement. I mentally shrug it off and raise her up. She starts to pull her arm out of the sling and I scowl at her.

"It doesn't hurt," she says a little more vehemently.

"I know, I just—"

"Mikah, please, it's alright."

"I know, I'm sorry. I just..." I pause. "I just really need you to get better. I don't want to see you do unnecessary harm to yourself."

"Honestly, all things considered, I feel pretty good. Just very tired."

I smile at her. "I will try and remember that. Now eat. Before it gets cold."

Maybe she really is mending that fast. Maybe those markings on her back play a great deal into her quick recovery, and maybe they're the reason the bleeding had stopped by the time I found her. Maybe they're even the reason she's still alive. Chances are good that Riley wouldn't have left her apartment until he thought she was dead.

I grab my BlackBerry and text Jack with one question: *Has there been any announcement regarding Vivienne from the police?*

I know that Elton was here, but he wouldn't know what kind of condition Vivienne is in. The only way he could know anything is if it has been leaked to the press.

I grab a bottle of water from the basket and open it for Vivienne, then grab one for myself and sit back down.

"Aren't you going to eat?" she asks.

"When you're done, I'll take from what's left. I want to make sure you get enough to eat."

"This will be enough."

"We'll see."

My phone chimes and I glance at it. It's a reply from Jack:

No. All they've said is that they are investigating the deaths of a police officer and a young woman. They've said that there is some information that suggests both are related, but that is about all at this point. Why?

"Is everything okay?" she asks me.

As I look up I realize that my brow is furrowed. I relax it quickly. "Yeah, just checking on a few things." I take a sip of my water.

"You don't have to stay." I can hear an underlying sadness in her voice.

"I have no place else to be other than right here. Unless of course you want me to leave."

She shakes her head quickly. "No, I want you to stay, I just don't want to keep you from anything."

I smile at her. "You're not. I'm trying to get some information on what has been sent to the media regarding you."

"Why?"

"Curious, aren't we." I smile.

"A little." She smiles back at me and takes another spoonful of soup into her mouth. "This is really good."

"Celeste is a great cook."

A scowl comes across her face and she looks up at me, confusion in her eyes. I can feel the tension and concern coming off of her.

"Oh. No, Celeste is my housekeeper. She's the one who put all this together for you."

As soon as the word *housekeeper* leaves my mouth, the crease on her brow disappears and her eyes almost glow. "Oh. I thought..." She turns away, back to her food, and takes another bite.

"That she was someone else?"

She nods.

I smile again. "No, Vivienne, there is no one else." *Only you*, I say, but only in my head because that is just too much right now.

She takes a few more bites in silence, then asks a question that catches me off guard. "Did you find me?"

Thirty-Seven

"What?" is all I can think to say.

"In my apartment. Did you find me?"

"Are you sure you want to discuss this?"

She nods slowly, hesitant.

"We can discuss this another time, Vivienne. We don't need to do it now."

"I need to know."

I take a deep breath, trying to decide if this is the time to do this. I'm not entirely convinced that it is, but if it helps her feel more at ease...

"Yes, it was me."

"How did you know?"

"That's complicated. I can't say for certain how, but I knew. I..." I pause and take a drink. Standing up, I walk toward the foot of her bed. "I'd planned to be here at the hospital when you got here for your appointment. I really needed to talk to you." I walk back to the chair and then back toward the end of the bed. The pacing helps me think about the best way to explain all this.

"So I didn't show up?"

"No, I...um, was running a little earlier than I planned, so rather than go to the hospital, I went to your apartment. There was a cab waiting out front."

"I don't remember calling for a cab," she says.

As I turn back toward the chair she is looking at me. "I think Dr. Alston had called for one for you."

"Oh. So what did the cab sitting outside have to do with anything?"

"Well, I assumed that you were still inside your apartment. Then, as time passed, I grew more and more concerned about why you weren't coming out." Back and forth I continue to pace, slowly. "So I called Detective Stevens."

Her head pops up at the name and a look of frustration and anger crosses her features.

I'm confused by her reaction. "What's wrong?"

"He was supposed to protect me." Her voice is small, but a hint of the tiger is in it. She's angry.

Anger surges through my body at her words. She's right – he was supposed to protect her, and he failed. "I don't want to defend Stevens, because I don't think he deserves it, but there were some unforeseen circumstances that got in the way of that."

Her eyes flare wider for a moment, as if she's remembering something.

"Do you know...?" She stops there.

"The cop that was stationed outside of your apartment was killed."

I watch as her eyes glass over. "Mr. Crowley, my neighbor. I remember Riley saying something..." She stops.

"I don't know anything about him," I say.

She takes a deep breath, steeling herself. "Why did you call Stevens?"

I can see in her eyes that she doesn't want to further discuss Mr. Crowley. I vow to ask Stevens or Jack about it.

"They came by my place Thursday night because of my car being near your apartment. That was when I learned about Rebecca's murder and the association between her and Riley. Stevens told me that you were under MPD protection. And then I knew that I needed – for my own peace of mind if nothing else – to be at your apartment to see you leave to meet Dr. Alston."

I continue pacing and I notice that she's stopped eating. "You have to finish your soup if you want me to keep talking."

She nods and goes back to it.

"The next few minutes in the story are a bit of a blur. I had Stevens call the officer that was stationed outside your apartment for a status update. When the officer didn't answer, I ran across Lake Street to the cop's car, only to discover that he'd been killed. That's when I went into your building. The rest, I imagine, you can figure out for yourself."

She finishes off her bowl of soup, takes a hunk of bread from the roll, and takes a bite, wincing as she swallows. She dips the bread into the bowl and soaks up the last of the liquid. She takes a smaller, soaked bite and then puts the rest down again. "I'm full."

"Are you sure? There is more soup."

"No, I'm sure."

"Alright." As I start to clean up, I finish my story. "I've been here at the hospital since they brought you in, and I've been in contact with Stevens, who will be anxious to talk to you."

"What's there to talk about?" she says sulkily.

I smile at her attitude. "Well, they're going to want to know what happened."

"There's not much to tell. I only remember little details." She is staring off at the far end of the room. "He

140

came up behind me just as I was about to open the door. After he pushed me inside and shut the door, he threw me down onto the floor." She takes a deep breath. "That's when my arm broke. I was trying to protect the baby by stopping myself from falling on my stomach."

My heart lurches in my chest. What she went through is just unbelievable, but I know I need to let her get it out.

"I passed out from the pain after he kicked me in the ribs." She squeezes the blanket in her hand so tight her knuckles turn white. "When I woke up next, I was strapped down on the bed, something over my eyes and mouth. My shoulder was in so much pain that I couldn't even feel my arm until I tried to free myself. My wrist was bound and broken."

I reach for her hand. She doesn't flinch or look at me, but she allows me to pull her hand away from the blanket and interlace our fingers.

"I don't remember much after that, other than something cool and sharp running along my chest. I think I passed out again. The next thing I remember is waking up here." She finally looks at me, and there are tears in her eyes.

I use my free hand to wipe them away. "You're alive, you're safe, and I will let nothing harm you."

"Have they captured him?"

I shake my head, and Vivienne begins to shake.

"Hey, hey, hey. Breathe, Vivienne. In. Out."

She takes a deep, shuddering breath in and lets it out.

"Slowly," I say. "I'm not going to let anyone hurt you."

I gently squeeze the hand I'm holding. The monitor beside me starts beeping. My head snaps up to see what is going on. Her heartbeat is erratic.

Then I hear the blood pressure cuff on her arm go off. She squeezes my hand harder.

"Vivienne, look at me." She turns to look at me. I smile at her. "Hi, darlin'. Take a deep breath with me. Ready?" She nods but I can see that she is turning pale. "In." I watch as her chest expands with mine. "Out." I watch as she slowly exhales and count to eight in my head. "Good, again."

We repeat the process again.

Then another machine starts going off. I look and see that her blood pressure has spiked.

Thirty-Eight

At the same time the blood pressure alarm goes off, I can hear commotion outside. A couple seconds later, the door clicks, and in walks Amanda.

"What's going on?" She looks to me.

"Keep breathing, Viv." I turn to Amanda and the door clicks again. Dr. Alston is standing in the doorway. "We were talking and she started to freak out. First the heart monitor went off, then after the pressure cuff was done, the next one went off."

"Vivienne, how we doing, sweetheart?" Dr. Alston asks from the foot of Vivienne's bed.

Vivienne seems to be on the verge of hyperventilating. "I—" Breath. "Don't—" Breath. "Know." Breath.

"Amanda, let's get her on oxygen. Vivienne, we're going to put a mask on you for oxygen and I need you to take some big, deep breaths, okay?"

Vivienne nods as Amanda brings the mask to her face.

"Deep breath in for eight counts. Deep breath out for eight counts. Okay?"

Vivienne nods again. I watch the monitor as she breathes in and out. Her oxygen level starts to climb, and I hear the pressure cuff go off again. Slowly her heart rate returns to normal.

"Good job," I say quietly so only she can hear me.

"Vivienne?" Dr. Alston says and we both look at her. "Good job. Do you feel better now?"

"Yes." Her voice sounds muffled coming through the mask.

"Okay, good. We can swap the mask out for a nose piece, but I want to keep you on oxygen for tonight, okay?"

She pulls the mask away from her face. "When can I go home?"

"In the morning we'll run a few tests and do an ultrasound. Once those are done and the results are in, I'll make that decision, but don't count on anything earlier than tomorrow afternoon. Once you leave here, though, you will be on bed rest until I see you again in two weeks."

"I can't do that," she says vehemently.

"You can and you will. I will see to it that you're able to manage things while you're off of work. Alright?"

"I'll lose my job," she says.

"Don't worry about that." As I say this she scowls and looks at me. The angry kitten is back, and I can't help but laugh. Always so feisty. A feeling of warm satisfaction ripples across my body. I sober quickly and add, "We'll take care of it, okay?"

Her scowl grows deeper, and this time Dr. Alston lets out a chuckle.

"Remember what I told you last time?"

She nods, and I'm curious what she told Vivienne the last time.

"Alright, Vivienne, everything looks good. I'm going to let you get some sleep tonight. I'll take off the fetal monitors so you can move around if you'd like. Push the button if you need anything." Vivienne nods and Dr.

Alston goes about removing the monitors and tucking them away with the machine.

"Is the IV still necessary?" Viv asks.

"After you finish the fluids that are in the bag now, Carol, your night nurse, can remove it. Okay?"

Vivienne's eyes shoot up to the two bags attached to the IV pole and scowls again. They only just changed them out the last time they were in here, and the bags are still about half full.

"Alright," she concedes.

"Good night," Dr. Alston says as she and Amanda leave.

"Good night," I say back. Turning back to Vivienne, I ask, "Do you need to go to the bathroom?"

She nods. I stand up, go to the cabinet near the TV and pull a blanket from the cupboard. Then I walk back to the bed, unfolding it as I go. "Lean forward, please."

She gives me a funny look but complies. I wrap the blanket around her shoulders and let it fall down to cover her exposed backside.

"Do you want to change while you're in there?"

"Uh huh."

"Okay, let's get you in there first. Then I'll bring your clothes. Put your arm around my neck."

She doesn't protest as I help her from the bed. But instead of letting her feet touch the ground, I pick her up. "Grab your IV pole."

She weighs next to nothing and I don't even have to adjust my balance as she shifts in my arms to grab the pole.

"Got it," she says.

"Okay." I turn toward the bathroom, savoring the feeling of having her in my arms.

She nuzzles her head onto my chest, settling in. "Thank you."

Without thinking, I kiss the top of her forehead. "You're welcome."

Thirty-Nine

After I get Vivienne settled back into bed, she falls asleep quickly - no doubt the day wore on her – and I take the opportunity to check my voicemail. It's full, and I quickly forward anything work-related, which eliminates about ninety percent of what I had in there. While clicking through the voicemails, I come across one from Stevens, left about an hour ago.

"Blake, it's Detective Stevens. Listen, I got a call from the hospital that said she was awake. How's she doing? Look I, um...I need to ask her a few questions and I will come by tomorrow sometime. We've gathered a pretty good mountain of evidence against Riley, including fingerprints from her apartment. Initial results on the blood found at the scene point to two different kinds. All we know so far is that they're different and one belongs to Vivienne. Once we know more, it may be enough to solidify the case against that idiot. We have a couple of leads on his whereabouts, too. I will let you know as soon as he's in custody. Please call me back at this number when you get a chance. I really need to speak with Vivienne."

Instead of calling Stevens back right away, I email Chrys, my attorney, requesting that he meet with me on

Monday at my condo to discuss representing Vivienne should this case go to trial. Knowing Chrys, this will not be outside of his area of expertise, and I'm confident that he'll be able to represent Vivienne well. Once that is done, I call Stevens back.

As I'm hitting send, a sharp buzz rings across my back, the same one I get anytime there is something to do with Stevens. Odd.

After three rings and a series of clicks, he answers. "Stevens."

"You called."

"Ah, Blake. How is she?" he asks.

"Alive. Torn up emotionally, but she's here and well as can be, all things considered." My tone is clipped. Her hyperventilating earlier has me on edge when it comes to Stevens. She's right: He was supposed to protect her and he failed to do so. Riley running free in the streets isn't helping my mood.

"I don't doubt that at all, but I'm glad she's awake. I planned to stop by tomorrow to talk to her."

"Don't bother. She has a mountain of tests in the morning and she will, with any luck, be discharged in the afternoon. You can wait until Monday afternoon, my apartment."

"You know I can't wait until Monday."

"You can and you will. She needs a chance to recover and get settled. On top of that, she needs a chance to speak with her lawyer before you get your hands on her."

"What does she need a lawyer for? She hasn't done anything wrong."

"No, she hasn't, but I'll be damned if I let that fucker walk out of a jail cell on bail again. Vivienne will have her chance for justice this time." I can hear the resolution in my voice and Stevens picks up on it, too.

"Speaking of justice, I received your recording. How in the hell did you get it?"

"Elton came to the hospital looking for me."

"You know that I can't use this in court, right?"

I roll my eyes. "That depends, Detective, on how you want to use the information. It doesn't exactly implicate Riley in the crimes, but it certainly indicates that Elton is fully aware of what his son was going to do and the reason for which he bailed him out of jail, don't ya think, Detective? Regardless, use it how you want. Use it to build a separate case against Riley or Elton. There's no doubt in my mind that if his lips are that loose with me, he will most certainly talk to someone else."

I can hear a heavy sigh on the other end of the phone. "I see your point. But Blake, it's in her best interest to give me a statement as soon as possible. The longer we wait, the more time there is for her to forget what happened or – as Riley's defense will say – for someone to tamper with her memory."

"Wait until Monday, Stevens. She's not well when it comes to what's happened to her. She started freaking out when I told her that he was still on the run. We don't need another incident like that one. Give it a rest until Monday, alright?"

Another heavy sigh. "Alright, Blake. Monday afternoon at your place." He pauses, and I can almost hear him consider arguing with me more, but in the end all he says is, "Thanks for calling me back."

"Yup."

I hit end before he can protest further.

Forty

"I would have talked to him tomorrow." Vivienne's small voice comes from behind me.

"Shit, I'm sorry, I didn't mean to wake you."

"It's alright. Nothing new?" I shake my head. "I'm alright. I know I'm safe here, and I know these things take time. The only reason he was arrested so fast the last time was because he left the apartment when he was done and a neighbor heard me screaming and called nine-one-one and I was whisked away to the hospital. When he returned to the apartment he found it without me in it and full of cops. At least that's what they told me."

"Fine. But that's no excuse for why they can't find him now."

"Sure it is. Riley has a lot of connections in this city. A lot of people will hide him, stand up for him, or defend him if necessary. Not to mention a few cop friends, too, who are no doubt keeping him up-to-date. Whatever you do, don't underestimate him."

"Do you know who those cops might be?"

"No, I don't. I don't really know much about his circle of people. He rarely ever brought business home, it was always done somewhere else. Which really sucked because when they arrested him, they wouldn't have

150

found any drugs around, nothing that could've kept him in jail longer." She takes a deep breath. "If they'd asked me about this before, I would have told them then, too, but I didn't have solid evidence that pointed to anything that would've helped my case against him, and I doubt even now I have any good information for them."

Wow, I think that is the longest speech I've ever heard her make, even when she was mad and yelling at me. "Well, I've put Stevens off until Monday. For right now at least."

"I heard. What's all this about your apartment and a lawyer?"

How can I put this so that she doesn't freak out again? "I, um, I emailed my lawyer asking him to meet with me Monday at my apartment to discuss your situation. I'd like you to be there."

"Do I need a lawyer?"

"I'd like to have one lined up for you in case this goes south and you either have to testify or press your own personal charges against Riley. Or both."

She's very stoic, no real reaction to what I've said. It's almost as if she's shut down. "I'll think about it."

I'm not sure I can take that as an answer, but I don't push her right now. I don't need her getting mad at me; I need her to know that I'm on her side so she'll agree to come stay in the condo I've had prepared for her.

She yawns.

"You're exhausted. Get some sleep. I'll be here in the morning and we can talk some more if you want."

She nods. "Thank you."

"For what?"

"For being here, for..." She pauses. "For rescuing me."

My heart swells nearly to the point of explosion at the tenderness in her voice. "I only wish I'd gotten to you sooner."

"Don't. I'm alive, my baby is alive, and you're here to protect me. That more than makes up for any mistakes you may feel you've made." Her voice is sincere and heartwarming.

I walk over toward her bed and lean down to kiss her forehead. Again she doesn't flinch, and I'm thankful for that.

"Thank you for your forgiveness." I lower the bed a little more. "Now, get some sleep. I'll stay off of the phone."

She laughs a little and closes her eyes.

Forty-One

I don't linger at going to bed myself, curious as to what the night will bring me. The dream I had earlier seemed to come to an end.

I settle into bed and, by the light of the bathroom I left on in case she needs it, I watch her sleep until I fall asleep.

This time it's different. I'm not in a white room. Or even a room that could be in Elysium for that matter. No, I'm...where am I? I know this room but I can't place it.

It's a bedroom with plush, light tan carpet and a king-size canopy bed made from a dark cherry wood with modern spindles made of what look like stacked blocks. The sheer white curtains flow down on all sides.

Someone is sleeping in the bed.

I walk toward it to see who it is. Sprawled out across the pillows is a mane of curly, bright red hair. It's the beautiful, pale, sleeping form of Vivienne.

I hungrily look her up and down and notice, under the blankets, the rounded baby bump propped up by something. Judging from the size of the bump, this is in the future, but not too far in the future. I come around to the far side of the bed to see her bare back. And it is covered in the same silvery and black wings as mine. *She really is an angel.*

I hear a noise behind me and I turn toward it. It's me.

What?

I watch myself move around the bathroom with a towel around my waist. The wings on my back are vibrant silver and black. On my right shoulder and extending down my right arm is the tattoo from the first dream. I'm shaving and brushing my teeth, the two things I usually do just before crawling into bed. It won't be long now; I need to get out of here before he sees me. Before *I* see me.

I look back to Vivienne, sound asleep on the bed. I could watch her sleep for hours: so peaceful, so angelic.

The light in the bathroom goes out. Crap. I look around quickly for someplace to hide, but it's too late; I'm already walking toward myself, looking straight at me. *Can he see me here?*

The other me walks straight through me and around the bed.

Nope. I back away from the bed as I watch myself climb in behind her, moving her hair out of the way so as not to lie on it. It looks a lot longer than I'm used to seeing it.

The other me wraps his arm around her and snuggles into her neck.

She moves, rolling backwards into him and turning so he can kiss her.

"Hello, beautiful. I didn't mean to wake you."

She laughs at him. "It's alright. I was missing you anyway." She smiles and kisses him. I watch as she reaches around his back with her left arm. His eyes roll. *She's touching his wings.*

Her motions have forced the covers down and her chest is now exposed. I feel a surge of excitement.

Sensing movement elsewhere in the room, I look up. Standing on the opposite side of the bed is Vivienne, just as she was when she left me in the last dream: beautiful, wings extended, and her hand resting gently against the swell of her stomach.

I look back at the couple on the bed. I now feel as though I'm invading their privacy, but I'm captivated by them.

I watch as I push the covers down further, exposing more of Vivienne. She's glowing - a white, blue, and silver aura around her, similar to the one I saw that first night.

Vivienne rolls over and straddles me - or him - and I watch intently as my hands roam slowly and softly along her breasts and her extended belly. I can feel my own arousal watching the two of them.

What happens next surprises me. Slowly the wings on Vivienne's back come alive and extend outward. It is an amazing sight to witness. Her wings are beautiful - white, with the slightest hint of silver accenting many of the feathers, and they shimmer in the dim light of the room.

I look past the Vivienne on the bed to the Vivienne standing opposite me. Her clothes have changed. She is wearing the gray, too-big t-shirt and black sweatpants I helped her put on before going to bed. I cock my head at her, puzzled.

Forty-Two

Suddenly I feel a tug, like someone is pulling on my shirt. I open my eyes and look up into Vivienne's shadowed face. "Vivienne? What's wrong?"

"I-I'm sorry, I can't sleep, I—"

"Come here," I say, and I pull back the covers. She slides in carefully, lying on her left side with her head in the crook of my shoulder. The harsh velcro of the sling rubs against my chest through my shirt. "Are you in?"

"Yes."

I wrap the blankets around us. "Good?"

"Uh huh."

As I start to pull my hand back from covering her up I feel her wrist brace against my arm, stopping me from pulling it back to my side. It takes me only a moment to realize that my hand is resting, open-palmed, across her bump. I have no words for the flood of emotions that wash through me.

As I lie here with her cascade of hair spread across my body, I contemplate how we got to this point. I can't imagine what's changed since I last saw her that has made her so trusting to the point of coming to me for comfort.

I snuggle into her a bit more. The warmth of her body pressed against mine is the beginning of an addiction I know I will never break.

Snuggled next to Vivienne, I think back to the dream I just had and the centuries-old story my mother used to tell me about *A chuid den tsaol,* or soulmates: the belief that there is only one person for everyone and that finding that one perfect person is rare. When you find yours, you know instantly because there is a bright aura surrounding that person; you will see it when you first lay eyes on them.

I think back to the night I met Vivienne, the night my back led me to her. Up until then, I'd had some indication that something was going on with my back, but I chalked it up to the old stories of the markings on my back and didn't make much of it.

I think I see now that it was a sign of what was to come: an omen, like dreams can be. Not like the dreams I've had these last few nights – nothing so overt – but something more along the lines of subliminal messages telling me who I am or what I would become.

The day I met Vivienne, my markings had been bugging me ever since I'd arrived at the site of the groundbreaking. As the afternoon progressed, it got worse, until it was so annoying I had to leave.

Just before I got in the car to go home, it was like my back took on its own personality, driving me toward my destination. Then, I didn't know why. But I'm sure now. It was driving me toward my *A chuid den tsaol.*

And now that I've seen parts of our future, I know that it is not just for her sake that I fight for her. It is for me, too. I can't imagine my life without her. She is as essential to me as air.

Is it possible that she is seeing some of the same things that I'm seeing? Is that why she's changed toward me?

While I know this battle is far from over, Elton made that very clear earlier tonight, I now know a glimpse of what the future holds for me, for us. Is that future set? Or is it up to me to protect her so that we get to that future?

Forty-Three

I can feel Vivienne moving in my arms, and my eyes open lazily to see morning light streaming in through the window.

"I'm sorry, I just have to go to the bathroom."

"It's okay. Do you need some help?"

"No, I think I'm okay."

"Okay."

She gets her legs over the side of the cot, stands up and starts for the bathroom, IV pole in tow. I'll be dammed – someone changed the bag. She's gonna be pissed. But I also notice – and it didn't register last night – that she is without the oxygen. I just shake my head. When she climbed out of her bed and into mine, she removed it.

No sooner does the bathroom door close than the door to the hospital room opens and Amanda comes in.

"She went to the bathroom."

"Ahh. How's she doing?" she asks.

"Don't know. I haven't had a chance to ask. We just woke up," I tell her, and she smiles.

I can hear the toilet flush in the bathroom and then the water starts running. A few moments later, the door opens. I haven't moved from where I was in the cot, and she smiles slightly when she sees me. I jerk my head in Amanda's direction.

"How are you feeling?" I ask her.

"Good. Tired, but good."

"That's good. Are you ready for some tests?" Amanda asks her.

"Um, no." She scrunches up her face. "Can we finally ditch the IV though?"

Amanda laughs, "Yeah. You fell asleep so she just changed out the fluids."

"I noticed. Can we please take it out?"

"Yes. Climb back up in the bed." Amanda says, and I head toward the bathroom.

"Don't go far, please?" I hear Vivienne ask.

"Nope, not a chance, just going to the bathroom."

She nods, but I see sadness on her face. I smile at her reassuringly.

I begin to wonder whether she feels the need to be near me because she feels safe with me. I take great comfort in this thought.

When I come out, Vivienne is IV-free and Amanda's pulling up Vivienne's shirt. I stop dead in my tracks and start to turn around.

"It's okay," Vivienne says. "She's just checking on the baby."

I smile and ask, "Are you hungry?"

"Famished."

"Can you wait a little until the tests are done?" Amanda asks.

"If I have to," Vivienne says sulkily.

My smile widens. "I'll call Red and have him bring up some food."

Amanda has finished revealing Vivienne's stomach. The little mound stands out even further than it did a couple of weeks ago. The sight is actually really sweet. Amanda puts a microphone-shaped thing on the bump, and almost instantly there is a rapid whooshing sound. The image of Baby Callahan's heartbeat on the ultrasound monitor the last time we were here comes to mind.

Vivienne's face lights up at the sound. She smiles and looks right at me, then smiles a little more brightly at my returning smile.

I don't know why I feel such a connection to her baby, but I do. I have this strange sense of hope that this is only the beginning of what's to come with us.

The whooshing sound stops as Amanda removes the microphone from her tummy.

"Sounds great, and I got one hundred and forty-nine beats a minute." She puts the equipment away and turns back to Vivienne. "Are you ready to go for a ride?"

"Can I walk?"

"No, you can either ride in a wheelchair or we can push the bed."

"Wheelchair then," she huffs.

"So feisty," I say, and she scowls at me. I stick my tongue out at her and she bursts out laughing. "That's my girl."

When Amanda comes back with a wheelchair, Vivienne slides down from the bed and sits down in it.

"Are you coming?" she asks me.

I look to Amanda, who shrugs. "That's up to you," she says.

"If you want me to, I'll come," I say, looking at Vivienne.

"Yes, please."

"Alright." I slip into my sneakers and fall in behind Amanda. "Can I push her?"

"Sure," she says and steps aside for me to take the handles on the back. "Follow me."

Forty-Four

We return to the room about two hours later to find that Red's already been here. He's left sandwich fixings – more of a lunch-type food than breakfast, but that's good because it's nearly noon anyway.

Vivienne's ultrasound went well, and Dr. Alston seemed pleased with what she saw.

Once Vivienne and I are alone, I put together a sandwich for her and she digs in. Probably not the best food on a weak stomach, but she dives in with gusto and I'm not going to stop her.

After a few bites she asks me a question I never thought she'd ask. "Why is helping and feeding me so important to you?"

I wonder if this is something that she and Dr. Alston talked about last time. I take a sip of water and swallow the bite of sandwich I'd just taken.

"My dad was not my father," I begin.

She looks at me, puzzled.

"My dad, Shannon, met my mother when she was about six months pregnant with me. When he met her, she was nothing but skin and bones, living on the streets of Dublin. Her own father had kicked her out of his

163

house when she told him she was pregnant, so she did what she needed to in order to survive.

"When she met my dad, he fought to take care of her. And of me." Wow, this sounds very familiar. I'd never thought about it like this. "He wasn't a wealthy man - he worked seventy or eighty hours a week to bring home squat for money and food - but he endured and managed to save enough money to bring my mom and me to the States. That's when things finally started to look up for our family. There were times when we all still went hungry, but the Irish community in Boston I grew up in was very supportive, and we managed to turn things around.

"My dad taught me that persistence, perseverance and determination drive any man to do the things they're good at. Mom taught me never to give up and to always help those that have less than you."

I look carefully at her. "Because of that and my mom's history, I'm a strong supporter of the shelters in Minneapolis and a big contributor to Hope House, which is a home for women, and specifically for pregnant women and their families.

"While I didn't know you were pregnant when I met you, I did see a young woman who needed a good meal and a new lease on life, which is why I left you that tip and refused to take it back from you."

I reach into my back pocket and pull out the now extremely wrinkled piece of paper wrapped around the cash still inside. "I've never opened this, and I never will. I brought it with me Friday with every intention of making sure you got it back. Now that you know the why, maybe you will accept it?"

My heart breaks to see the shiny wet spots on her cheeks. "Oh, Vivienne, don't cry. Please."

"I feel so stupid. I feel like...I feel like if I'd accepted your help when you offered it, not kicked you out of my hospital room...or if I hadn't even shown up at your office that day-"

She sniffs and I reach for a Kleenex. "I feel like had all that not happened, I wouldn't be here. After I kicked you out, Dr. Alston said that you really were just trying to help me. That it was a no-strings-attached kind of help and that I might be overreacting to your generosity." She wipes her nose and the tears from her face with the tissue I hand her.

"But at the time, I was so determined to prove to myself - and only myself - that I could do all this on my own. I realized very quickly that you both were right, but I didn't know how to swallow my pride and call you."

I'm not entirely sure what to say to her speech. I'm completely blown away. "I understand what it means to swallow your pride. It's not easy, and I understand why you couldn't. I'd planned to be here on Friday for your appointment, hoping that I could convince you that all I was really trying to do was help."

"I understand that now," she says. "But you also need to understand where I'm coming from, too. I've spent so much of my life without a parental figure, struggling to survive everyday...but somehow someone was always there to pick up the pieces. It was never my mom, it was the little old neighbor lady. Or Riley." I watch as her face distorts on his name.

I cock my head at her and she takes a deep breath, as if having decided something. "After my mom had her stroke, I was homeless, with nowhere to go except school and a little cubby inside my old apartment until I met him and he basically took me in." She shudders. "I grew up in a house full of drugs, alcohol and abuse. It turned out

Riley was no different, though instead of doing drugs, he dealt them. And that is something that I will have to deal with the rest of my life."

"What if I told you that I would never let that happen to you again?"

"Mikah." The sound of my name on her lips sends flutters through my body. "You can't take care of me forever. I'm not your burden to bear."

"You're not a burden, and please do not ever let me hear you speak of yourself like that again. I give my help freely, Vivienne, and without strings. You and I both know that you can never go back to that apartment. So where are you going to go?"

Forty-Five

She doesn't answer, and I know she is contemplating her options and how few they are. But I need her to answer me. Finally she says, "I can go back to the shelter until I can right myself again. I've done it before, Mikah, I'll do it again."

My heart breaks. "No, you won't. I will not let you struggle to make ends meet. I won't let you roam around the streets of Minneapolis, and I will not let you be alone. Viv, please. Understand that I cannot walk away from you. I care to much about you."

She is crying again, but she doesn't argue with me.

"Look, Viv, I won't force you to do anything you don't want to do, but I ask that you consider something for me."

She nods slightly through the tears.

"I have a condo by the river. In my building I own three units - mine, Red's, and one that was meant for Celeste, my housekeeper. Celeste refuses to live in the unit. I want you to take it."

"Mikah, I can't..."

"Please, just hear me out?" I ask, and she nods. "Alston said yesterday that you won't be able to return to work for a couple of weeks. How are you going to make ends meet if you aren't working?"

"So this would only be for a couple of weeks?" she asks.

"If you wish, but let me finish. The apartment is yours, to do as you wish, decorate how you like. My crew is at your disposal. When the time comes and you can return to work, I want you to come work for me."

"Doing what, Mikah, I have no skills. That diner was the first job I've ever held longer than a couple of weeks."

I'm taken aback by her rebuttal - not because she is arguing, but because she is devaluing her abilities.

"I have an entry-level administrative assistant position for you. It will pretty much be answering phones, taking messages, making copies, things like that. It's easy, relatively stress-free work, and more importantly, it comes with a salary you can live off of. You won't have to be on your feet, and it would even offer medical benefits so that you can pay your own way for the things you need if that is what's important to you."

"What about the apartment? There is no way that I can afford it, even with a salary."

"We can work out a lease. You can pay me rent every month, if that's what you need to do to feel comfortable."

Her brows pull together. "How long do I have to think about this?"

"Until you're discharged, but know this: I will not allow you back into that apartment, period. And I will not allow you on the streets or anyplace where Riley can track you down. So until he's caught and this matter is resolved, I need you to come and stay where I can be close to you, keep an eye on you."

She doesn't answer me but nods, acknowledging that she's heard me. I didn't expect an answer from her, at least not right away, and I don't get one.

Forty-Six

The room has been completely silent for a while, and the loud click of the door makes us both jump. Looking toward the door, we see Dr. Alston coming into the room.

"Am I interrupting?" she asks both of us.

"No," we say in unison, and Vivienne smiles, giving me hope that she's not upset with me.

Dr. Alston laughs. "Well, okay then. Vivienne, I have some good news."

"Yay! Do I get to get out of here?"

"I'll get to that. First of all, your shoulder and wrist look great. I will let you take off the sling, but I'd like you to wear the brace for at least another couple of days. You can take it off to shower, but put it back on when you're done. Okay?"

"Okay, is that all?"

"Eager, aren't we?" Dr. Alston smiles at Vivienne. "Your lung is still healing. While the outside is nearly completely healed, which is nothing like anything I've ever seen before, it's still a bit inflamed. But it's nothing that will keep you here in the hospital."

"What about the baby?" I ask, and Vivienne looks to me for reassurance.

I move closer to her, hoping to provide a little more comfort, and she surprises me by putting her hand on my back. I feel a rush of pleasure through my body that has to do with something more than the fact that she is touching me, and I realize that she is tracing her fingers absently along my right wing. When her fingers cross over to normal skin, the difference in the sensation is marked.

"The baby is doing fine. You're measuring a little bigger than fourteen weeks, but clearly that's due to the fact that you've been eating more food." She looks pointedly at the remains of Vivienne's sandwich on the tray. "What with the unnatural rate at which you're healing, I'm not going to be concerned right now about weight.

"Also...I didn't ask you during the ultrasound because I didn't want to get you worked up, but I was able to determine Baby Callahan's sex, and I've taken the liberty of putting the proof in here." She pulls out an envelope from her pocket. "I've never been wrong," she says a little smugly, "but it's not guaranteed. And I'd rather you look when you're ready to find out. If you choose not to look, well, it will be a surprise when you have the baby."

"Okay," Vivienne says, taking the envelope. "I'll let you know next time whether I've decided to look. Now can I leave?"

Dr. Alston rolls her eyes. "So impatient." Then she asks, "Where are you going to go?"

My ears perk up and my heart sinks, dreading the answer.

"I can't discharge you unless I know you're going somewhere safe," Dr. Alston continues. "Hospital policy. Do you have something set up?"

She nods.

I grow hopeful that she will take me up on my offer.

"Mikah has offered me a place to stay for a while, until I can get back to work and on my feet. I'm going to go home with him."

YES! I shout inside my head, and at the same time Vivienne gently pats my back, right between my shoulders. I have the sudden thought that Vivienne has been in my dreams with me.

"I think that is a great idea. I've scheduled an appointment for you for two weeks from tomorrow at ten. And no working at least until then, okay?"

"Yes, ma'am."

"Okay, here are your discharge papers." She hands Vivienne a stack of papers. "You cannot walk out of this hospital – it is a liability – but someone will come with a wheelchair to get you in a little bit. That'll give you a chance to get packed up, and then that's it, you're free to go."

"Thank you, Dr. Alston. For everything."

"You're welcome, Vivienne. It's what I'm here for. I rather look forward to seeing you under happier circumstances. I will be in touch in a couple of days to see how you're doing. I'll see you in a couple of weeks, but feel free to call me if you need anything before then."

As soon as the door closes behind Dr. Alston I turn to Vivienne. "Thank you. For not putting up a fight about my request."

She lets out a breathy laugh. "Yeah, 'cause you gave me so many options. But in the end, you're right, I really have no place else to go, and I'd much rather be closer to you."

I lean over and kiss her forehead. "Thank you, thank you, thank you."

"For what?"

"Giving me hope."

Sneak Peek

Do you honestly think I would leave you hanging again?

Give Me Desire - Available NOW

Reason Series Book #3 - AVAILABLE December 31, 2013
Visit Zoey's Author Page on Amazon:

VIVIENNE CALLAHAN, discharged from the hospital after surviving a near-fatal attack from Riley, her abusive ex-boyfriend, has come to the safety of Mikah's protection. As she continues to heal physically and mentally from her ordeal, she begins to have strange dreams...dreams that follow her into waking life and hint at a fate she never could've foreseen and dangers far greater than Riley.

Meanwhile, MIKAH BLAKE has some ideas about her future, too, and the more she considers his proposals, the weaker her resistance to him becomes. His recent actions have taught her to respect and trust him, but soon her feelings for him threaten to deepen into something more, something she may not be ready for.

In the third book of the Reason series, Vivienne will discover who and what she and the people around her really are.

*** Sneak Peek at Give Me Desire ***

"Do not toy with me." His anger radiates off him in waves and the temperature in the room rises.

"It is done, Master. I've completed the task you've assigned me." He does not look upon the other man's face as he speaks. He's kneeling some distance away, causing him to shout to be heard.

"Get up!" The evil voice fills the room, stunning everything inside.

The young man stands but does not raise his head.

The scene changes, and instead of a small, dark room, they are in a cavernous one, with strange pockets of steam rising through cracks in the rock floor. Somewhere nearby echoes of the hollow screams of tortured souls can be heard.

"Your job was simple, you were to kill her. Here you stand, not only her blood but the blood of at least two others on you. And yet I do not believe you have completed your task, minion. Why is this?"

"I don't know. I left her dead, she was dead when I left." He begins mumbling – low and incoherently - and twitches as though he can't stand his own skin.

"Ah, but she is not dead. If she were dead, I'd have all my powers back, and..." Suddenly the room is lit up by a bright white flash. The air is instantly charged, static making hair stand on end, and the young man crumples to the ground. "And I'd be able to kill you."

"No! Don't. Don't hurt him," a female voice says, and a girl runs from behind a rock to be at the young man's side.

"Who are you?" the dark, mysterious man shouts.

"What are you doing to him?" She looks down at the crumpled form on the floor and reaches out to touch his dirty blond hair. Looking up in the direction of the voice. "Who are you?"

A deep, throaty laugh comes from the man in the shadows, making the hairs on the back of her neck stand to attention. "I am your worst nightmare, child."

The echo of heavy footsteps across the rock floor fills the cave, each step getting closer. She cowers, trying to pull the young man with her, but she fails. She lets him slump to the ground as she scrambles backwards on her hands and feet.

"What are you going to do to me?" she whispers breathlessly. Her body shakes in fear.

There is no response as the shadowy figure keeps walking closer with slow, measured steps.

"It is not you I wish to harm, child. It is this boy who needs a lesson in obedience." There is an edge of reverence in his voice, as though he's longing for something.

"What are you going to do to him?" she asks, the fear dropping away from her voice.

"If he'd done what he was supposed to do, I'd do nothing to him. But he has failed me and he deserves to be punished, perhaps tortured." The voice is menacing and yet also strangely enticing to her.

"Take me instead," she says, and she rises to her feet.

The footsteps stop. "What would I want with you, girl?"

"Anything, everything. Let Riley go and take me instead."

"Tell me your name, child." It comes out a growl.

"Nyssa."

Acknowlegements

THANK YOU!! From the bottom of my heart I cannot thank you all enough for your amazing support!

I'd like to first thank my editor - Sione. Your patience and unyielding words of encouragement mean the world to me. Thank you for all your amazing hard work and dedication to this project.

My Son deserves so much credit here! He puts up with Mommy writing, Mommy stressed out, and without that patience, I wouldn't have been able to finish this project.
My Mom - I love you with all my heart! Your support and encouragement knows no end. Thank you for everything you've done.

Barb, Rachel, and Vickie - Girls, you sure do know how to keep me on track, your subtle and not so subtle hints are well received, I'm working on it, I promise!!

The Z-TEAM!! I HEART YOU GUYS!! Your love of my writing is inspiring and I look forward to many more adventures with your guys!

To my fans and friends - I HEART YOU ALL SOOOO HUGE!!

Thank you Thank You THANK YOU!!

About Zoey

Amazon Best Selling Angels, Demons & Devils and Paranormal Author of Give Me Reason - The Reason Series Book One comes from Glendale, Arizona. Zoey, was a mortgage underwriter by day and is now a paranormal, romance and erotica novelist full-time. She writes stories as hot as the desert sun itself. It is this passion that drips off of her work, bringing excitement to anyone who enjoys a good and sensual love story.

Not only does she aim to take her readers on an erotic dance that lasts the night, it allows her to empty her mind of stories we all wish were true.
Her stories are hopeful yet true to life, skillfully avoiding melodrama and the unrealistic, bringing her gripping Erotica only closer to the heart of those that dare dipping into it.

The intimacy of her fantasies that she shares with her readers is thrilling and encouraging, climactic yet full of suspense. She is a loving mistress, up for anything, of which any reader is doomed to return to again and again.

On Twitter: www.twitter.com/ZoeyDerrick
On Facebook: www.facebook.com/Zoey.Derrick.1 -
Personal
www.facebook.com/Zoey.Derrick (Author)
On Her Website: www.ZoeyDerrick.com
Email Her: Zoey@ZoeyDerrick.com